TALES OF
ENCOUNTER

TALES OF ENCOUNTER

THREE EGYPTIAN NOVELLAS

Yusuf Idris

Translated by
Rasheed El-Enany

The American University in Cairo Press
Cairo New York

First published in 2012 by
The American University in Cairo Press
113 Sharia Kasr el Aini, Cairo, Egypt
420 Fifth Avenue, New York, NY 10018
www.aucpress.com

Dar el Kutub No. 2230/12
ISBN 978 977 416 562 7

Dar el Kutub Cataloging-in-Publication Data

Idris, Yusuf, 1927–1991
        Tales of Encounter: Three Egyptian Novellas/ Yusuf Idris; translated
    by Rasheed El-Enany.—Cairo: The American University in Cairo Press,
    2012

        p.   cm.
        ISBN 978 977 416 562 7
        1. Arabic fiction
        2. Arabic fiction – Translating into English
        892.73

1 2 3 4 5   16 15 14 13 12

Designed by Nora Rageb
Printed in Egypt

CONTENTS

MADAM VIENNA

can almost picture Mustafa, or Darsh, as we used to call him, standing in his familiar way in that vast square, about which he knew nothing except that it must be one of the squares of Vienna, which he knew to be the capital of Austria. More importantly, he was conscious that he had been there for two whole days, paying five pounds per night for the hotel without getting anywhere.

The square was not really vast. In fact, the largest Viennese square would not measure up to the smallest in Cairo. Anyway, a square it was, bordered by ancient imposing buildings, decorated with countless friezes, and painted in solemn brick red, as if specially selected to suit the semi-dark atmosphere in which the people of the north lived. They were buildings that you felt were inevitably built by Europeans; Europeans with red complexions from drinking wine; and whose eyes were small, blue, and cunning.

Darsh, as is clear from his name, was an Egyptian citizen who traveled to Europe as people do, on the face of it for official business but in reality for recreation and sightseeing. He was a civil servant in the Ministry of Trade, who for more than six months had left no stone unturned to have the official mission concerning commerce with Holland assigned to him and not one of his rival colleagues. He emerged victorious and was chosen. Thus he spent many days ceaselessly moving between the passport office, the finance department, consular offices and embassies, and the district registrar's office in order to have his travel documents in place. He boarded trains and ships until he arrived in Amsterdam and successfully accomplished his mission. And here he was now in the heart of Vienna, which is probably a good moment to lay bare a secret about our friend, Darsh, that he has been keen to hide. The truth is he has not come to Europe for the official business. Not even for recreation and sightseeing. He came for only one reason: women; his innermost desire being to try the charismatic European woman, having had his fill of conquests among the women of his own country. Mind you, that was an overstatement: Darsh could never have his fill of women.

He has a respectable appearance: tall and handsome; easily the most elegant in his department. In the corner of his mouth he has a large black birthmark, he's well-shaven with no moustache. He has a light brown complexion, but black curly hair. Serious and composed, he exudes self-confidence when he speaks to you, and would always call you 'love,' even if you're a stranger to him. He's a true Egyptian, who never misses an opportunity for joking or repartee, and in no time at all he's looking at you from the corner of his brown eyes, saying, "Come on! Don't be stupid!" And like any Egyptian, when angry he would say to you, "I swear I will tear your eyes out." He'll be furious and demonstrative but the least gesture will appease him, however, the one thing he won't tolerate is for someone to try to take him for a ride.

Darsh at work was very different from Darsh in his private life. His reputation at work was all-important to him and he stuck to the rules and treated people well, though this did not, of course, stop him from occasionally telling off those under him and occasionally flattering those above him. Married with a young daughter (after the manner of the personal columns of our newspapers), Darsh has one hobby that he practices in such complete secrecy that his closest friends would be dumbfounded to find out about: women. So adept and artful is he at this hobby that from one glance he could tell which paths led to a woman and how long it would take to ensnare her, and whether that would be by ignoring her, by being over-attentive, or by playing Don Juan. Indeed the art of seducing women is a multifarious one. You've got those who specialize in blondes, brunettes, maidservants, movie stars, or school girls; even old women have their seekers. As for Darsh, his specialization was in a variety completely different. He liked raw women: his heart's content was to be the first conqueror of a woman. That's where his genius lay. He would deploy all his art in leading on such a woman step by step, slowly like a skilled and patient hunter who relished all stages of the hunt. His wide experience in the field gave him unlimited self-confidence, so much so that he used to say to us, "The problem is not how to ensnare a woman, but how to get rid of one."

Darsh had then finished with Egyptian woman. His intention now was to conquer Europe, the woman. From the moment he set foot on the gangplank of the ship, there was a restless gaze in his eyes, as if he had lost something for which he was looking in the face of every woman that his sight fell upon. It is true that during the journey and his stay in Amsterdam he made the acquaintance of a few women, but circumstances had always been against him; there hadn't been a single opportunity. Amsterdam in particular was awash with visitors from everywhere, come to celebrate an occasion about which he knew nothing. But in this throng of many thousands there did not arise a single chance. This did not, however, concern Darsh in the least, because he was a man of style, and there was no way that the feverish atmosphere which swept over Amsterdam during the festivity would allow him to savor the experience the way he wanted. But he knew where he could get his heart's desire. He had met some of his fellow countrymen, knowledgeable in this department, and wasted no time in being open with them. They in turn were straightforward in their advice: "If you want women, my friend, go to Vienna!" In fact, Vienna was his target even without their advice; Vienna of whose companionable nights Asmahan sang in her sweet, sonorous voice. Whenever he listened to that song, he would quiver with boundless dreams, dreams that perhaps were among his most important motives to undertake this journey.

And there he was in Vienna. Two days he has been there. In fact, this was his third night in the city of companionability and dreams and nothing has happened despite the fact that women are all over the place, Austrian women in whom the spirit of Europe was concentrated, women of different forms, colors, and ages, and all without exception beautiful in no small measure. Even the ugly among them had beautiful bodies or enjoyed a refined taste in dress. Each possessed something, something of Europe; each had something special about her. His attention was divided, scattered, and his eyes, as at the beginning of the journey, were unable to rest on his prey.

It was eight o'clock in the evening and the square was lit. Everything in it was lit. Above the highest building in the square, there was a news ticker announcing the latest news, its lit words scrolling in a language he did not understand. He was the only one, though, staring at it; the only stranger with no news from home since he left. He made out the word Egypt and his heart pounded with excitement: it must be that the display is mentioning something that happened there. Immediately an image of Egypt lit up in his mind, the whole of Egypt and everything in it that belonged to him. The image vanished almost as soon as it appeared, but it left him ashamed and ill at ease, as he stood in the square still scanning it with his gaze for a woman.

Finally he started to move. He had been roaming the city on foot for two days now. He would loiter in front of shop windows and drink filter coffee for which he could never develop a taste. And he would attempt with women all the tried and tested techniques perfected back home, such as faint smiles accurately beamed, or certain glances noticeable only by the targeted woman. Or he would sometimes claim ignorance of the bus fare and pick the prettiest passenger near him to ask her. And to be fair, not a single woman that he approached was anything but the epitome of courtesy. Not one snubbed him. They would smile to him charmingly, guide him with exactitude, and answer his questions with impeccable politeness. Sometimes he would try to surprise one or other by blurting out that he is Egyptian, and they would genuinely be astonished and say, "Really? How exciting!" But then the astonishment would fade away, and the cold excuse-me smile would flicker on the woman's lips, as she gracefully walked away. They had deceived him, no doubt! Those scoundrels who said to him, "All you have to do is march up the street with your brown skin and curly hair for women to be falling at your feet. Or just say you are Egyptian and it's a done deal!" Well, he had said it a thousand times and nothing was afoot.

He kept circling the square aimlessly, unable even to venture further ahead, as that was the only square from which he could make his way back to the hotel. He certainly did not want to get lost in a foreign city, especially considering that all he knew of foreign languages were the few words of English that he still remembered from his student days in the Faculty of Commerce, and a few sentences in French which he used to rattle off by heart in secondary school, such as "*Tous les bateaux de tous les pays sont ancrés dans le port*" and "*Ali Kamil est un élève doué à l'école secondaire.*"

Suddenly he found himself at the other end of the square. But that was no accident. He had spotted from afar a woman standing by herself, and hastily made his way in her direction, praying silently she would not move or a companion appear. Thankfully, when he reached her, she was still alone. Not just that, but to his surprise, when he was close enough and smiled to her, she smiled back.

"Good evening!" he heard himself say.

"Good evening!" she said in English, almost laughing. Her German accent sounded strange to his unaccustomed ears.

He was overjoyed and felt he had made a giant leap forward. He stood in front of her and asked her the time. "A silly mistake," he immediately told himself. "You could have started the conversation more intelligently." But it turns out he was in no need of any intelligence.

"What does it matter? Let the time be 10:00 p.m. or 1:00 a.m.! It doesn't matter," she answered as she swayed.

He realized that she had been drinking and found that strange, because she looked young, hardly sixteen. She was very pretty with delicate innocent features and a pleasant attitude. Her body undulated before him like jelly. "She is drunk and beautiful and can hardly hold herself together. What are you waiting for?" he thought to himself.

He drew very close to her until their bodies touched. He laughed wickedly and said, "Would you like to join me for a drink in that place over there?"

"Sorry, I can't," she replied.

"Why not?" he asked.

"I'm waiting for my boyfriend."

He was disappointed. "But where is he?" he asked.

"In the toilets," she said as she pointed at the lit entrance of a subway nearby, probably leading to the toilets.

"Forget about your boyfriend! Come on, let's go!" he said with characteristic Egyptian bravado as he took her by the arm.

But she refused as she tried to wriggle out of his grip. "I can't. I'm waiting for my boyfriend and I can't abandon him," she protested.

"But I find you so attractive," she added after a moment, "that I want to kiss that pretty mole of yours on the side of your mouth."

Her remark pleased him and instigated more bravado. He pulled her toward him with a little force, beginning to feel excited.

"I'm here and your boyfriend isn't. Forget about him and make do with me!" he urged.

She was pliable in his hand, like dough, but did not budge. Meanwhile, he saw a man climbing the stairs leading from the subway, and he let go of her hand. The man continued in their direction. Darsh felt ill at ease and withdrew a little from the young woman.

"Good evening!" intoned the young man coldly, as he put his arm around the girl's waist and led her away, "Let's go, Teddy!" The girl staggered away in her drunkenness. She did not so much as look back to cast a glance on Darsh, who stood there in a state you would not wish on your worst enemy.

His transfixion, nevertheless, did not last for long. He soon resumed his wandering in the square, almost in despair. He was terrified that as it got late the square would empty of people, especially women, as happened in the two previous nights. But the square did not empty and women were anything but in short supply. That was not Darsh's real problem. The real problem was if he were actually to make the acquaintance of a woman, what was he to do, being unable to take her back to his hotel? The concierge was a sour-tempered man, not at all the type who would allow such a thing. Where then would he take that putative woman since it was unlikely she could take him to her place? Maybe she would be able to show him another B&B or hotel where they could go together, but that would require their acquaintance to have cemented sufficiently, while he wanted all that to happen in one night, nay, in a small portion of a night. How on earth could he make the acquaintance of a girl and become close enough with her to be able to take her to a hotel in the course of an hour or two? What was even more important was that he did not want a streetwalker; he had

11

already turned down a lot of soliciting as he walked the streets of the city. What he wanted was a decent European woman, a woman of character who wanted him, not his money, and who would give him herself of her own free will. It was indeed a well-nigh impossible situation.

Suddenly he started to notice something. The square began to fill with sailors, young men aged seventeen to twenty, yet dressed in naval uniform. From their accent he realized they were American. Vienna wasn't a harbor: where did those sailors come from? He found that a hard question to answer. Perhaps they were on furlough? On a European trip? Everything was possible. Be that as it may, it was clear they were roaming the streets like him, individually and in cliques. He could see some black men among them and was astonished to find them more brown than black: he had always imagined American blacks to be pitch black. All the sailors were young and no matter what color their skin was—white, brown, or black—they all had the same look in their eyes: like him, they were looking for women. "Okay! Let's see what's going to happen, Americans!" he thought angrily. Out of the blue he was confronted with hundreds of rivals who, like him, were looking for women. But on second thought he felt reassured: the type of woman he was looking for was different from that sought by those young sailors. He was searching for Europe, the lady, while they were after the frivolous Europe. And what a difference between the two! For some reason, however, he did not expect them to meet with much success, because he was of the opinion that European girls, too, must be resentful of the new American imperialism and that they would make an honorable stand against those frolicsome sailors.

But to his surprise and in no longer than half an hour since the sailors appeared in the city, every one of them was already in the company of a young Austrian woman. How did they do that so quickly? And where did all those women come from? A real mystery! Moreover, they seemed already to be on intimate terms: he could see the young sailors' hands reaching for the girls' waists and necklines in no innocent manner. It must be that those 'foreigners' communicate with each other in ways that we Orientals did not understand. It was only natural that groups of sailors and young women began to form, walking with their arms around each other's waists, drunk and boisterous, singing and dancing in the streets, uninhibited.

Then the noise began to subside and the young people began to break into pairs, each fading into a dark street, in the direction of the park, the nightclubs, or other semi-deserted streets in order, of course, to engage in activities not permissible in the light. All this in view of Vienna's solemn elders who wore dark-colored hats and serious faces, and its aged women in their black dresses. All this they witnessed without raising an eyebrow, as if it were not happening in their own city and to their own daughters. As if it were the most natural of things.

Darsh was sizzling with anger at the Viennese. But even at the height of his disapproval, he was not unaware that he too had been looking for a woman and that some of his

anger was caused by his failure where the Americans succeeded. "I won't feel better until I've had a good couple of
beers," he thought to himself, even though he did not like
beer, nor alcohol in general, the taste of which he actually
hated. Nevertheless, he walked into the nearest bar after
making sure it was not too chic: he had been bitten before.
He ordered a beer from the old barman, casting a furtive
glance at the bill as he was served. When he saw the price,
he decided that his first glass was going to be the last too.
He started to drink, while making a conscious effort to be
happy. He was in Europe, he told himself, spending a
beautiful evening in the enchanting city of Vienna. Yes, all
that was really happening to him, and he ought to enjoy
every minute, nay, every second of it, for tomorrow all this
will turn into a memory of the past. But the harder he
tried, the more chagrined he felt, the more lonesome. And
being at the bar did nothing to ameliorate his feeling of
loneliness. It was the same scene as in any bar: a call girl
sitting near the door; a balding middle-aged man with a
little paunch sitting at a corner table with a woman of
similar age, looking at each other affectionately while two
glasses, still full, stood between them; and at the bar, the
only source of some noise in the place, stood a bunch of
men, near him, among whom was a middle-aged woman
with a long cigarette holder between her lips, laughing
loudly and acting young. It was obvious that here, too, he
was not going to find his heart's desire.

When he left the bar, the beer had gone to his head.
He had begun to feel that his shyness, his fears and worries

and complexes were retreating to a corner of his mind. In fact, he was beginning to be possessed by a crazy desire to throw all reserve to the winds: in a country where no one knows you, anything goes. Thus he began to throw around evening greetings in a loud mirthful voice to the right and to the left as he walked, not caring whether anybody reciprocated. And if a woman turned her face away in disapproval, he would stick his tongue out, as if saying, "To hell with you! Do I have to be American to win favor?"

The Americans were by now few and far between. It would seem that it was time for them to report back, and their new girlfriends were seeing them off at bus stops. Some of them were badly drunk and causing a racket. Those who were still sober were practically carrying their drunken mates into taxis. He began to witness farewell scenes between the sailors and the girls, mostly light-hearted, interspersed with kisses. But there was also one touching scene: a young black sailor and a short blonde Austrian, every bit a schoolgirl. They stood at the tram stop for an hour, her hand in his, their eyes locked in a never-ending gaze. Darsh stood opposite them watching in amazement: could love be born and flourish in an hour? We must indeed be living in the nuclear age.

Darsh would wait until an American had left and then he would follow his girlfriend, not feeling in the least uneasy about his behavior. But even in his slightly inebriated state, he did not try to approach any of them. He wanted first to be noticed and shown a sign of acceptance, however slight, before advancing. He did not want to be humiliated even in a country where no one knew him. But the girls seemed keen on hurrying home, as if satisfied and desirous of no more.

When the cathedral clock struck twelve, the square had emptied completely of the sailors and the young women; only a few clusters of pedestrians were still waiting for buses and trams. There he was once more alone with Europeans, the people of Vienna, without the rival Americans. But the freshness of early night brought him no cheer. Despair was creeping over him relentlessly. It was the same story as in the two previous nights when he had to return to his hotel alone through the familiar narrow streets to retire, heartbroken, to his bed. All indications were that tonight was going to be no different.

Once more Darsh started to wander about the square reviewing the faces of passersby and those standing waiting in the hope of hitting upon his goal. So many lookalike faces, as if duplicates of one face. Noses sloped from foreheads at the same angle, and eyes were almost all of the same color and reflecting the same gleam. Those were people who knew each other and understood each other, and their German language with its *Nacht* and *fucht* and what not traveled between them like an electric current carried by hidden wires, tying them together, uniting them, making them one large homogeneous body, while he stood apart with his strange color, nose, hair, and language: he alone was the odd one out. This was by no means the first time that he was seized by a nostalgic feeling for his country.

Every time he smelled sausages being fried, heard German babble of which he did not understand a word, or was snubbed by a woman he was staring at, he would feel a pang of nostalgia for his city, his cute little apartment on Ibn Khaldun Street, and his wife, as pure as the prayers of dervishes around the Mosque of al-Husayn; his wife who at that very moment was sleeping deeply, dreaming of his return and waiting for him, exactly as she had done every time he came back home from his late-night outings with his friends like a disobedient son. He would also feel nostalgic for his little teething daughter, and particularly her two little front teeth, which showed every time she complied with his request, "a kiss for Baba," and her little slippers that he had bought her a while ago and whose red woolen uppers have frayed, while the soles remained intact, having never touched the ground. And yet here he was, in the heart of Vienna, looking for a woman to try her European flavor. And it was past midnight. So what? He shook his head violently as he walked, as if to shed off those thoughts. Nothing could stand between him and the thing he wanted and for which he had worked hard for a whole year. He had done the impossible to get where he was now—was he going to waste his chance now? He knew he would feel guilty, very guilty. But he must seize the opportunity here and now. Later, when he was back in Egypt, there would be time enough to suffer the pangs of his conscience. But now there was no time left. Minutes raced away off his watch at a crazy speed and the night marched on relentlessly.

17

In a corner of the square he glimpsed a group of young women who looked pretty much like the girls he had seen earlier with the Americans. He approached cautiously before stopping short to watch the scene from a distance with a mixture of outrage and pity. In the midst of the group was a young man who looked for some reason like the boss. He stood erect, head raised, and was dressed in the manner of latter-day Austrian thugs: tight trousers that narrowed substantially at the ankles, and a short leather jacket. On his head, he wore the mark of the age—pompadour hair—and in his eyes was an exaggerated insolent look. He was barely twenty, yet he was engaged in a charged argument with the girls and two friends of his. Darsh's ears picked up a few words: Americans, dollars, and a variety of insults in English and German. It was clear that the argument was about 'business' and a serious disagreement over profit. What a disappointing ending to the story of his honorable rivals, the American sailors!

Before long, the heated argument had turned into a brutal brawl, at which point Darsh decided to stop watching and move away completely from that miserable square, come what may. After a short consideration he chose the broadest street branching off the square and headed in its direction. The city center had not yet emptied of people: there were still a good number of pedestrians around. A light drizzle had started, and Darsh hesitated whether or not to wear the cheap plastic raincoat he had specially bought to protect his smartest suit from European summer showers. If he wore it, that might make him look less handsome in the eyes of women. If he didn't, his best jacket, that only the day before he had paid a fortune to have dry-cleaned, might be ruined. In the end he preferred to play it safe and put on the coat.

All shops in the street had their display windows lit; windows full of goods that the heart of every traveler desired: cameras, tape recorders, lighters, delicate artifacts, and much more. Darsh was in a crisis. On the one hand, he felt a pressing, almost irresistible desire to inspect the contents of those windows and to compare the prices with those of Cairo in order to choose the best value for money. And yet he resisted for two days because it came down to one of two things: either he gives himself wholly to that or to the 'mission' for which he came to Europe. His suffering as he walked the street was almost visible: the commodities on display, at which the Viennese deployed all their art in decorating and arranging them under the night lighting, simply dazzled him at a time when he was already hardly in possession of his senses, with his attention riveted on what pedestrians there were. It was as if he had four eyes, each assigned with a specific task: one for the immediate section of the pavement on which he walked and another for the opposite pavement, while a third looked further ahead in anticipation and a fourth focused on stretches already traveled in case something had been missed by any of the three other eyes. The first task was to distinguish the gender of the walkers from their clothes, and when it began to rain, the focus turned to umbrellas to sift the male from the female. Once gender was established, the next step was to determine age: old women were discarded like men, and so were pubescent girls. Women suspected to be prostitutes were also rejected. Thus he was left with a very small percentage on which to focus his attention. All this meant that the way he progressed along the street was most peculiar. He would be walking on one side when suddenly he would cross over to the other side. Or he would be walking in one direction when suddenly he would turn around and retrace his steps; all of which changes energetically synchronized with frequent movements of taking off and putting back on his cheap plastic raincoat. If he recognized a female in the approaching figure, he would take off the coat. But if she turned out to be the wrong type, he would wear it again, and so on and so forth.

Thus when Darsh noticed an indistinguishable figure approaching from a distance, he prepared himself for all eventualities. He took off the plastic coat, patted his hair in place, and slowed down his pace into a graceful and dignified step to indicate character and power. He was right: the approaching figure was indeed that of a woman. Not only that, but also of the required type. Darsh, however, was not very hopeful about a sudden change of fortune. He crossed the street to the opposite pavement where the woman was and walked in her direction. By now he had become so adept at recognizing female beauty from the least evidence, and it was clear that the woman approaching was not a stunner. She was nonetheless good looking with an elegant walk and a certain tilt of the umbrella she kept open even after the rain had stopped: only a beautiful woman took extra care of her clothes, her makeup, and everything related to her appearance.

He tried to attract her attention while she was still a few steps away to give her a good chance of seeing him, but he failed: she only noticed him when they became right opposite each other. While he ogled her, she cast on him the merest inconsequential glance; that typically European incurious glance that he had grown accustomed to. She did not possess the beauty of which he had dreamt. Almost his height, she wore a beige wool coat with a high collar. Contrary to the prevalent fashion, she had long thick hair. She had a kind face, but handsome, too, with nothing for makeup except lipstick, or at least so he thought. She did not wear a smile but she did not scowl either. She would make an excellent housewife, doctor, or maybe a cellist in a second-rate orchestra.

Intent on trying his luck, Darsh turned around and started following her. When he was close enough to be almost abreast with her, he hesitated whether he should go past or continue to follow her. He opted for the latter to remain master of the situation. The woman walked ahead for a while until she turned into a side street. Darsh followed on, and as her steps grew more hurried in what turned out to be a quiet street with few pedestrians,

Darsh realized she must have suspected she was being followed. And although he had no idea what the chase might lead to, he nonetheless sped up too so as not to lose sight of her, mindful at the same time of his direction and road signs to be able to retrace his steps after he had failed. Yes, for he was pretty certain he would fail. As to why he was persisting in his endeavor despite certainty of failure, this may lead us to the contemplation of human nature. When mankind despaired of success, they tended to make up for it by persistence. One failure is just that, but numerous failures may pass for partial success.

Be that as it may, Darsh thought it was time to speak to the woman. He stepped up his pace until he was abreast of her. He swallowed and asked her, in a polite, docile voice and with an English accent that he did his best to polish, the way to the Hotel Sacher. That was a question he certainly did not need to ask, since first he was not staying at the Hotel Sacher, a top-rank old hotel where your feet sank in the plush of authentic Persian carpets, way out of his league, and second he knew very well the way to the modest Hotel Victoria, where he actually was staying. By asking the woman, and all those others before her, that question, he had a tripartite purpose: to convey that he is a foreigner, rich, and lost. By so doing he thought he would be opening the gate wide in front of any woman, even the least inclined to adventure.

The woman's reaction took Darsh by surprise. She turned her head away as if afraid. But by the time he was finishing his question in a more self-confident tone of voice, she seemed more self-possessed. Or perhaps not quite yet, for it was well past midnight, the street dimly lit, the question incomprehensible and was being asked by a stranger. In hardly coherent English, she explained that she had not understood.

For the third time, Darsh repeated his question, coming close to giving up and walking away: a woman so alarmed at being asked a question was not likely to have the stomach for adventure. But it was at that point that her features eased up into a smile. "*Ja, ja*," she said in a serious tone, and started to point with her hands and umbrella as she tried to explain to him in stammering English how to get to the Hotel Sacher. Darsh understood nothing, but pretended otherwise as he followed her explanations nodding energetically. Meanwhile his well-trained eyes were busy reading her features in search for that certain something that he knew perfectly well, and which a woman's face transmitted when she wanted the man in front of her. But there was nothing. Her expression was serious, and her enthusiasm to help him find his way genuine. Nothing more. Finally, and with that cold smile that he had become accustomed to, she excused herself and went on her way. In turn, Darsh threw all her directions to the wind and followed her. He tried to detect in her gait the signs that her face had denied him: some hesitation perhaps or irregularity in her footsteps as she realized he was still following her despite her directions. Again nothing. But when the woman reached a policeman standing at the corner of the road in his usual helmet, she stopped and said something fast to him in German, pointing at Darsh who had fallen back at some distance and started to prepare himself for any accusation with which the policeman might confront him.

So there was no difference between an elegant Austrian lady in Vienna and a lower-class woman in Cairo: both would report him to the first policeman. That was what Darsh was thinking when the man approached and greeted him with a polite smile before beginning to describe to him in sound English the way to the Hotel Sacher. Darsh's heart began to beat normally again. The woman was innocent. It was evident she thought he had followed her because he had not understood her explanation, and she just asked the policeman to try again. Impatiently Darsh listened to the policeman's long and polite direction, all the time his eyes restlessly following the woman's movements to be able to continue to follow her once out of his predicament.

Indeed no sooner had the policeman turned his back, than Darsh headed toward the side street into which he had seen the woman turn. And so pleased with himself was he, when soon enough his ears were able to pick up the rhythmic sound of her high heels against the cobblestones of the street. But only at that moment he realized that the thing he most feared had happened: this time he had really and truly lost his way. What on earth was he going to do now with those similar buildings in similar streets with similar names? He knew he was going to be lost for as long as it pleased God.

But he was not too worried. If worse came to worst, he would only have to take a taxi and let the driver ask what he would of Austrian shillings, each costing more than ten Egyptian piasters. Nor was the irony of the situation lost on him: he had been stopping women to ask them the way to the hotel, which he knew very well, and now the pretext had turned into reality and he was lost in earnest and in need of genuine help. And wouldn't it be nice if that help came particularly from the woman that he was following, and whose footsteps rang sweetly on the cobbled street in the tranquillity of the night in a way that stirred up his longings, and left him after each clang waiting in excitement for the next.

But sometimes he would sober up and accuse himself of madness for arranging everything so tidily in his mind, when the fact of the matter was that the woman, like all the others, had not shown the slightest interest in him. Only one thing was sure: he was going to fail. And even if, for argument's sake, he ceded that he might succeed in engaging her in conversation, what use was that when the time was so late and she could only be on her way home? And again if the impossible were to happen and he could make an appointment with her to meet the following day, what could happen then apart from sitting in a bar or café; an unsavory French coffee for him and an exorbitantly priced drink for her; and maybe a few squeezes of the hand, and then nothing.

Nonetheless he was adamant that he would succeed with that woman or another that night, and that he would spend with her some very good time somewhere nice. An impossible mission, perhaps, but he felt it was imminent and held fast to it. For some reason he was certain that what he wanted would come to pass: it was the same kind of tenacity that brought him to Europe in the first place; the same kind of strange tenacity that characterizes us Egyptians. The tenacity one sees in the famished father, who can barely keep a roof overhead, to bring up his son with the fly-infested eyes to be a doctor or engineer. The tenacity that one finds again in the fellah who wants to irrigate a vast area of land, using the primitive shaduf, which lifts no more than a palmful of water at a time from the irrigation canal. What is really amazing is that that tenacity actually pays off. The father will wrestle with his fortune, his poverty, and his class until he makes a doctor or engineer of his son; and the fellah will bend and straighten up a thousand times, nay, a million times, until he succeeds in irrigating the land.

Such too was Darsh's tenacity. The distance between him and the woman he had been following was contracting in measure to the expansion of his ideas and plans for her. He decided that the best course of action was to cross over to the other side of the road, outpace her, cross back and bump into her face to face and then see what happened. He did exactly as planned and within a few steps of her, he stopped, simulating surprise. "Here we are again!" he said, "It's a small world!" She too appeared surprised, though her face remained neutral as she continued walking without word or gesture.

In response and only two steps later, Darsh made the firm decision immediately to head toward the main street and take a taxi back to the hotel. Enough was enough! The woman now probably thought he was deranged, and would surely call the police in earnest if he pestered her again. His decision, however, endured for only ten steps, after which he turned around and started to follow the woman again, this time leaving a wider gap between them to be on the safe side. On she went and on he followed. He thought he had been following her for dozens of kilometers, but his watch told him it only took a few minutes. Eventually, the woman emerged from the narrow street into a small square, not unlike the Khazindar Square in Cairo with an enormous store occupying one of its sides. Around the square scattered a number of tram and bus stops and an odd mixture of people wanting to catch the last service. The woman stood at one of the bus stops, while he continued walking, looking left and right, up and down, in the manner of someone trying to figure out something. Finally he arrived at the same stop to stand at some distance from the woman. He remained still for a moment, then changed his position and put his hands in his trouser pockets and looked ahead in a certain direction like someone waiting for something and walking up and down meanwhile. He kept shifting his position and movements in a self-conscious way, as if he were accountable to an unseen force that watched his every stirring and demanded justification, when in fact nobody in the square noticed him. Not even the woman he had been following, who stood leaning on her umbrella, betraying no expression except for the anxiousness typical when waiting for a tram or bus that seemed never to come. Eventually Darsh was within a step or two of her. Exactly what he had been maneuvering for. Now what? He pushed his hands into his pockets and took them out several times, looked this way and that, and fixed his gaze in her direction for a long time, hoping their eyes would meet. But in vain. He had to do something more radical. Thus he approached her in a state of complete indifference and stopped in front of her, a big smile on his face. "May I ask you a question?" he said.

"I'm a foreigner, as you can see, and I don't speak German," he continued without waiting for an answer. "It's a great opportunity for me that you speak English. Would you mind if I asked you a few questions about things here?"

As he finished his question, he was overcome by a genuine feeling of embarrassment, and was unable to meet her eyes again until he heard her say, "What do you want to know?"

He looked up at her with renewed hope. True, there was a smile, but it was entirely devoid of meaning. At any rate, it was better than a scowl or a telling off. He had to make up his mind about that woman fast: it was either a "yes" or "no"; he had sufficiently made a fool of himself already. But first he had to ask her about what he wanted to know. And so, he inquired about the time of the last tram, which sounded to him sillier than anything he had said in his life. But she answered with the same meaning-less smile, "A quarter to one."

He felt even more clumsy. A change of plan was nec-essary. "Actually, I only wanted to talk with you a little, would you mind?" he said. And before she answered, his mind was processing the new situation fast. There was no doubt that she had recognized him as that for-eigner with black hair who asked her the way to the Hotel Sacher, and who did not care to follow her direc-tions but followed her. That meant that she was not angry with him; that she was not put out by him follow-ing her. Or maybe it was just curiosity that made her listen patiently to those silly questions of his. Maybe it was that curiosity too that painted that meaningless smile on her face.

"Not at all," came her reply.

"She is ready to talk," he thought. "Speak, Darsh! Speak!" He tried hard to find something to say, and after a silent moment in which he tried to summon all the powers of his silver tongue, he could not do better than, "I bet you don't know where I come from."

"Of course not," she said.

"Can you guess?" he said with a smile.

She was silent for a short while before she said indiffer-ently, "Portugal?"

He nearly reacted with a boisterous Egyptian guffaw before he remembered he was in Europe. "No," he said.

"I don't know," she said resignedly.

"I'm Egyptian," he said boastfully.

"Really? How strange!" she said.

He was annoyed, even though she had said it in the most casual of ways and did not seem to impregnate it with any particular meaning. But he dwelt on her words. "What's strange about it?" he asked.

But she said nothing in reply. She just maintained her expressionless smile, showing no desire, apparent or hidden, to continue the conversation. He felt that if he carried on, every additional second would be at the expense of his dignity, and that the best thing to do was to call it a day and go.

"Thank you. Nice meeting you!" he said and walked away.

When he found himself at the other end of the station, he started thinking again. It might very well be that she had only spoken to him out of a sense of curiosity, but if she had been unwilling to speak to him, she would have made that plain somehow. Why didn't he continue talking to her? And what was stopping him from trying again now? But how? Under what pretext would he go back now, having said goodbye and left? He had better have an intelligent excuse this time. He retraced his steps.

"I hope I'm not intruding," he said when he had reached her. "But if you don't mind, are you sure that the last tram is at 12:45?" As he talked, he studied her face, and felt a trifle reassured when he saw there was no disapproval of his return or his stupid question, which he had intended to be clever.

"Yes. At 12:45 exactly," she said. "And if you want to go to the Hotel Sacher, you can take a bus from the bay over there; it should be here in a few minutes."

"Thank you very much," he said.

He was silent, but he did not budge. Nor did she change her expression, or move either.

"Austrian, aren't you?" he asked suddenly.

"Of course!"

"Waiting for the bus?"

"The tram."

"Going far?"

"To the suburbs."

"Is that far?" he said in a desperate attempt to keep the conversation going.

"Half an hour," she said.

"Oh! That's long," he said with exaggerated surprise.

His next thought was, "Take it further, come what may!"

Thus he started to talk to her the kind of talk he had perfected on the ship, the trains, and in the hotels where he lodged; the kind of conversation that normally took place between any foreigner and any native. The weather—how lovely it is in Egypt, and how terrible in Europe in the winter; Austria had fallen under occupation but was now independent, just like Egypt; Egyptians liked Austrians; we too heard about Egypt and the Egyptians, and so on.

Throughout the conversation, and amid the questions and answers and jokes, Darsh's sixth sense, a one-hundred-percent sexual sense in his case, dedicated to picking up any positive signal from women he was trying to engage—that sixth sense was hard at work, trying to pick up the most fleeting emotional response: a look, a movement, anything. But nothing! He was utterly unable to penetrate the reality of her attitude: was it a yes or a no? It was as if her features too were inscribed in the German language, which he could not understand. He even thought that she could have talked in that very same manner to anyone at all, even if he were not a foreigner with curly black hair like himself. Such was his bewilderment even though she had started to smile, laugh, show surprise, and appear to listen with interest as the conversation went on.

Darsh was annoyed. Although he had inwardly settled for a chat with her until her tram arrived and she was gone, he was still annoyed by her impenetrability. He was so vexed, he felt he couldn't care less if he said something to make her angry. After all, it was just a few moments he was spending with her, never to see her again. Let the worst happen then! For here he was at long last and after an arduous effort standing close to a genuine Austrian woman, talking to her and making her laugh. So reckless did he feel, he nearly asked her if she would accompany him to his hotel.

But he did not. For at that moment her tram arrived. He stood there as she, her smile unchanged, pointed to him the stop from which he could take the bus to the Hotel Sacher. She climbed into the well-lit tram with a few scattered passengers, while he remained standing on the platform, not knowing what to do. He looked at her through the tram window, and she looked back and smiled too. He waved goodbye to her, and she nodded in acknowledgment; all of which meant that everything was finished, that their brief encounter was over, and that they had to go their separate ways.

But suddenly he found himself mounting the tram and sitting next to her. She looked alarmed, but not as alarmed as he had feared.

"But this tram isn't going in the direction of the Hotel Sacher," she said, "it's going in the opposite direction."

"So?" he said with a mischievous Egyptian smile.

"Where are you going then?" she said, surprised.

"I'm going where you are going," he said after a little hesitation.

"But I'm going home, in the suburbs," she said, her face betraying some concern.

"All right then, I'll go with you."

"Forgive me! Your behavior is rather odd," she said looking more concerned.

"Forgive *me!*" he said, escalating his Egyptian frivolity, "it is not odd behavior. It is in fact the behavior of a madman."

Her concern turned into fear. Or more accurately the beginnings of fear. She shrank in her seat and fell silent. It was the silence of helplessness. For what could she possibly say or do?

Darsh of course was neither odd nor mad. He was only acting on instructions from his gut feeling. Or that sixth sense of his that had gone into overdrive. The woman's attitude had not changed in any way that could justify his new tactic, but he was acting like those oil explorers whose equipment told them if they dug in that spot, they would find black gold. For him too there was something. Something deeper than his feeling, his thinking, even his intuition, that called to him to persist, to continue on the road to the end. His road, like the tram route, consisted of stops. And there he was, past the first stop, riding next to her. He had now to find out what more stops there were. But how to know? And where to begin?

"So, you're going home?"

The tram had started to move, and she was looking out of the window. She looked at him as if she had not heard his question. When he repeated it, her answer was just a glum, "Yes."

Her serious tone annoyed him, but he went on to ask slyly, "You live with your family?"

"Yes," she replied innocently.

"Married, I think?"

"Of course."

He was on the point of saying, "Me too, and I have a little girl with red sandals and two front teeth." But he stopped short. No need to complicate matters. Instead he asked if she had children.

"Yes. A boy and a girl," she replied, her indifferent smile returning to her face for the first time since they came onto the tram. If she didn't want me, he thought, she would just have said yes and stopped there, but she went on to count the children, which meant she wanted to go on talking. His next thought, however, was that parents were always pleased to talk about their children and never tired of it. Maybe he should continue with this line of conversation. Perhaps it would lead somewhere.

"What ages are they?"

"Tommy, the elder, is six, and the younger, a girl, is only six months."

Great, he thought. She was talking and that was a good thing. Her eldest boy was six, which means she was about thirty. Great! A mature woman who met all the conditions. Darsh's conscience could have moved at that moment to remind him that he was talking to a married woman who was also a mother, and that what he wanted out of the conversation was something unscrupulous. But Darsh's conscience never stirred on such occasions. He only believed in one law that governed the world: the law of what he wanted. What he wanted defined what was legitimate, what was right. If what he wanted was difficult to attain, or belonged to someone else, or any such thing—those were matters that were of no concern for Darsh. His one and only thought for the time being was how to continue the conversation without interruption.

"Please don't take offense," he began, "but something is bothering me. Women where I come from don't go out alone at this late hour of the night."

She laughed, which he found reassuring.

"I went to the opera with a friend. That's all."

"I thought you were a working woman," he muttered

as if to hide his embarrassment, "and that you were kept late at work."

"I finish work at eight."

"So, you do work?"

"Of course," she said.

"How wonderful!"

"Actually most women work here."

"I know, I know," he said, thinking hard about his next question.

"But if you go on like this, you will be getting very far from your hotel," she suddenly said.

"It doesn't matter," he said, smiling.

"Where are you going to spend the night then?" she asked, truly surprised.

"It doesn't matter. Anywhere," he answered, unconcerned.

She shrugged and went back to looking out of the tram window.

This meant that the conversation would descend into silence—silence that was his greatest foe. He had to go on talking. So agitated was he that he began to swing his leg nervously, if unnoticeably. His sixth sense had betrayed him, no doubt. Not only was the woman a wife and mother but her manner of speaking and the way she carried herself showed her to be sensible and prudent. Everything pointed to failure: he should despair. Already all his movements, thoughts, and even looks were beginning to fall prey to despair. Already he was beginning to come to his senses and consider getting off at the first stop and starting his uncertain journey back to the Hotel Victoria. He only had to say something to bring the conversation to an end and exchange names and telephone numbers, for up to that moment he had not learned her name nor she his. Thus she would join a myriad of similar encounters that ended in names written in clear script in his pocket diary together with telephone numbers and addresses. Names of persons whom he already knew he would never meet again or correspond with. Yes, he had to finish his conversation with her now by any means.

"Are you really married?" he asked her almost unintentionally.

"Of course," she said laughing as she turned her face away from the window, "don't I look married?"

"The truth is," he said flatteringly, "you don't look in the least bit married."

Feeling her approval of the compliment, he continued, "Seriously, are you really married and have children?"

"Of course!" she said stifling a laugh, "Haven't I already told you that? I am married, but . . ."

Darsh's heart leapt inside his chest, and he held his breath waiting for what might be behind that 'but.'

He did not have to wait long. "At present," she continued, "I don't live with my husband."

His heartbeats raced, loud, excited, and joyful. And he laughed. Just like that without reason. The kind of laughter with which we hide our emotions. The reason for his elation was not that she did not live with her husband, but because she had told him. If she did not want him, she would not have told him. She would have just told him that she was married and kept that irrelevant detail from him.

He was still in seventh heaven when she looked out of the window and said, "This is Leopold Platz: you are getting very far from your hotel."

"It doesn't matter," he said throwing his head back.

"If I were you, I would get off at the next stop," she said, "you may still be able to catch the last bus back."

"It doesn't matter."

"Where are you going to spend the night, then?"

"I know very well where I'm going to spend the night," he said lowering his glance while looking at her, and stressing every word in an attempt to impregnate the words and glances with maximum meaning.

She gave up and fell silent while retaining her smile. He was silent too for a while, as he started a series of furtive motions in his seat to bring himself closer to her. Whether she had noticed or not, she held on to her silence. Darsh, for his part, was transported to a world of wonderful dreams. Until now he had only learned that she did not live with her husband, yet he felt sure he was going to spend the night with her: it was a done deed. And thus his greatest dream, which moments ago had looked almost impossible, had come true. With incredible ease. The very dream that had brought him over to Europe—he was now living it. And next to him was the woman he had always imagined. Next to him in the flesh and smiling. He observed her closely. At leisure. As a cat did a mouse, having captured it. He was happy to observe her. Happy to devour her with his glances and to delve deep with her into his dreams. No one could have blamed him for wanting to stay like that for a while, lost in his inflamed imagination, rather than continuing straightaway his effort to possess her.

But an unexpected thought interrupted his dreams. It occurred to him that it was odd for the woman to be married and not living with her husband. With his usual impulsiveness, he turned the thought into a question.

"Forgive me if this sounds like prying into your affairs, but why doesn't your husband live with you?"

She was slow to answer. And although he had known her only for a few minutes, he was already able to interpret some of her reactions. He realized that her reluctance meant that she felt uneasy and that he should not have asked that question. To save the situation, the delicate thread that tied him to her and which he did not want severed because of a crude question or improper word, he went on to ask her what kind of job she had. She told him that she worked as secretary for the director of a major company that manufactured electrical equipment.

"Oh! I see. That explains why I feel so *charged* sitting next to you," he said surrendering to his Egyptian sense of humor and in an attempt to lighten the atmosphere.

"Be careful! You might get a shock," she said laughing.

He was beside himself with joy to hear her comment.

"There's nothing I wish more than to get that shock," he said, drawing closer to her.

Her tut-tut, by way of reply, made him squeeze himself even tighter next to her.

"I definitely need another shock," he said.

All that happened against embarrassment on both sides: half-said words, eyes avoiding encounter, and the like. From that moment Darsh appeared to treat her as if he had known her for a year. Caution was thrown to the wind. He no longer cared what he said or how she took his questions. But in reality he was only pretending. Deep inside, he was still perplexed. Still uncertain if she had accepted him or whether what he saw of her was normal behavior that could never lead to what he dreamed of.

As usual Darsh decided to leave the matter for events to determine the outcome. Her stop was no doubt approaching and he intended to get off with her. It would then be up to her.

And so it was. In a few moments, she began to prepare for getting off. "I shall have to leave now," she said.

He smiled and said nothing. He thought it wiser not to tell her what he intended in case it led to an argument he could do without. All he did was to get up when she did and get off when she did. He had expected any reaction of her except what actually happened. She said nothing when she saw him get off the tram and walk next to her. She just shrugged smiling.

"Where are you going?" she asked a moment later. He made no reply.

"Where are you going?" she asked again.

Again he made no reply. Action, not talk, was going to decide the matter. Thus he took her hand in his and they walked together. Everything proclaimed that she had no objection to him going home with her. Nevertheless, he did not feel secure. He could not believe that everything had gone so smoothly. It was just beyond belief.

"Is it far to your home?" he asked casually.

"Just around the corner over there," she said.

He was overwhelmed by a sudden attack of bewilderment. Was this woman an innocent angel, or a sly witch? Did she like him, or was she making fun of him? Put your arm around her waist and let us see what happened, he thought. He was incredulous when in return he felt her arm go around his own waist.

"Is there anyone at home?" he whispered throatily.

"Of course: my children," she replied.

"How old are they?" he asked forgetting he had already been told.

"Haven't I already told you?" she retorted, "Tommy is six years old, and the youngest is a six-month-old girl."

"Shall I tell you something?" he said, "I'm coming home with you."

She smiled her neutral smile, and shrugged. That shrug which could mean 'no' but could also mean 'yes.'

What must be done must be done, he thought, kiss her and see what happened! If she was happy, you could put your mind at ease. If not, a rethink would be needed.

Slowly he raised his hand from her waist until it reached her neck, then he stopped her, turning her around to face

41

him. He embraced her tightly and kissed her on the lips. He never knew what she thought of his kiss, nor whether she was content or angry. She was still for a moment then pushed him away gently as she said, "You are going to break my back, African." Her words made his already overheated blood race even faster in his veins.

The street on which they walked was long with very tall lampposts on either side. It reminded him of the Cairo road leading to Heliopolis. As he walked alongside her, he felt for the first time since meeting her that she was his for the night. And for the first time he felt reassured about the outcome, and that there was no need for haste or impetuousness. He should act with the self-confidence of a predator that had its victim lying still under its paws.

But something began to nag him. A little thought that came from nowhere: why did the woman accept his advances so easily? It was clear that she was not a woman of loose morals. She didn't even seem to have known any man other than her husband. There was even something not one hundred percent feminine about her. She had the hallmarks of working women: the way she walked and talked. Even her smile betrayed a serious, forthright woman of the world, used to dealing with men on equal terms. Why then was she putting up with him?

These thoughts raced up in his mind, casting doubt on the situation. Perhaps his sense of confidence was exaggerated. Perhaps the woman was totally innocent and it was he who portrayed things the way he liked. His fears made him want to make sure: he held her even tighter and put his lips to her neck and started nibbling her until he felt her quiver under the heat of his breath. He then lifted his lips slowly to hers and kissed her. To his surprise she held him tightly and kissed him back.

"I want to kiss you again," he muttered.

"Me too," she muttered back.

His blood boiled over in his veins: this is how a woman should be. In the east, women are lifeless; they can only be had against their will, even when they are head over heels in love with you. They are only pleased if taken by force. But here when you kissed a woman, she kissed you back; when you embraced her, she embraced you; when you took her, she took you. This is how it should be. Such was true gender equality. He took her hand and started caressing it, feeling a gush of intimacy and tenderness for her. He felt her slender fingers, strengthened no doubt by the constant striking of typewriter keys. The touch of those fingers made him feel a strange collegiality with her.

"Is your house far?" he heard himself ask her.

"Just a little way ahead," she replied.

They had walked quite some way. The street lamps were now at longer intervals and the darkness denser. Contrary to what he expected, Darsh felt strangely at home with the darkness. The night was like a vast curtain drawn over the street. Over the whole of Austria. The whole of Europe. Almost making him forget that he was a stranger in that land.

They walked on for quite a bit more with nothing on her features to indicate they were getting any closer. Darsh was beginning to feel anxious. Things between them were at high temperature that was only likely to drop the longer the journey. They might begin to have a conversation, which was in their situation undesirable, indeed quite detrimental.

"You must live at the end of the world," he said.

"In this case, we've just arrived at the end of the world," was her reply.

He laughed and so did she, remarking that the house was at the next turning. Darsh was relieved as they actually turned after a few more steps into a little side street, which though narrow was lined by two rows of very high trees, maybe those pine trees about which he had learned in geography lessons at school. The street was exclusively residential, consisting of closely situated low-rise houses. They kept walking until they reached a huge apartment block.

"I live in the block on the right," she said pointing at the building. "Can you believe that all this is owned by one proprietor?" she added.

That comment made him feel that she was trying to hide something. Maybe by 'one proprietor' she meant the government. Maybe those were tiny flats built by the state for low-income families. How foolish she was to think he cared even if she lived in a shack. It was *her* that mattered. She led him into the third block whose entrance crowded with a not insignificant number of bicycles.

"Which floor?" he whispered.

"Just here!" she said, as she climbed a few stairs to the first floor, stopping at the door facing the building entrance.

It all felt unreal for Darsh. He must be dreaming. But no he wasn't. Because she had stopped at the door, turned the key in the keyhole, and pushed the door open. Inside, the apartment was not dark: it was faintly lit by an electric lamp. Darsh felt afraid: maybe this woman was one of a gang who lured people, especially strangers like him, to murder them, as Rayya and Sakina used to do in Alexandria. A silly thought perhaps, but what if it were true? He stayed near the front door of the flat pricking his ears and intent on a swift escape if he heard any talk or suspicious noises inside. But he heard nothing. Meanwhile, she had disappeared. Rather than ask him in, she had disappeared inside: she must be up to something.

"Why don't you come in?" she whispered, "Do come in!"

His heart beat. This time without fear. He walked in so cautiously. As if on the edge of a cliff. She walked in front of him in her normal step without fear or caution, which he found strange.

The hallway was small and neat with not a square inch of its space left unused. Despite the dimness, he was able to take stock of the furniture pieces and their state: they were not new, but they did not look worn out either. The hall, the whole place, had a special smell, that smell of a small family home when you enter it for the first time; as if every family had a special smell, felt only by a visiting stranger.

"Aren't you going to shut the door?" she said in a whisper from afar, nearly loud enough to pass for normal talk.

In his awkwardness, he had forgotten to close the front door of the apartment. When he tried, he did not know how and she came to his help.

"Don't make any noise!" she said.

He hardly needed that instruction: he was already too disoriented to make any noise. The whole situation was so strange for him. Not because she was married, for he had known many married women in the course of his life, but he had never met a married woman in her own home. Nor was he perplexed because he felt he was defiling the sanctity of a home, or the sacred bond of marriage. Such concepts were totally foreign to his private moral code. Only the situation was unusual. Completely novel. That was the explanation for his racing heartbeats. The strangeness of the situation heightened his excitement. For there he was, not only having a European woman, but having her in new, exhilarating circumstances.

She walked through a door at the end of the hall, opposite the front door. He understood that he had to follow her. As he crossed the hall, his ears began to pick up a faint, rhythmic sound. He stopped and listened for a while. It was the sound of snoring, no doubt. It came from the room on the left with the half-closed door. He smiled like a child. The snoring was little and thin and low-pitched like a kitten's. It must be one of her children. She came out of the room she had entered.

"Why haven't you come in? Is something the matter?" she said, not trying this time to tone her voice down into a whisper.

"Nothing. Nothing at all," he said awkwardly. The fact was since they entered the apartment she had turned into a different person. She had become more at ease, more practical, more daring. Perhaps because she felt she was on her own ground. As for him, he was no longer in control. He now had to wait for her to make her move before he responded. He was now the one led, held in awe of everything, shifting his gaze from one thing to another, as if all things stared at him to catch him red-handed.

She walked back into the room, and cautiously he followed her. It was immediately evident that it was a bedroom. Her bedroom. On one side there was a bed. A strange bed that was neither single nor double, but something in between. As if made to accommodate a person and a half. Next to it was a table on which dozens of things crowded: an alarm clock, medicines, toiletries, books, brushes, knitting needles, razor blades, and other unimaginable things. Against the opposite wall was a swing cradle, in which lay a baby. It was difficult to tell if it was a boy or a girl.

"This is little Viola. She is six months," she said observing he had been staring at the cradle.

"Really?" he said in amazement.

The baby was big. As big as his own eighteen-month-old daughter. Amazing people, those Europeans! Their children are always healthy and plump, while ours are always suffering from tummyaches, diarrhea, always wrapped up and fearful of the evil eye. More important, however, than the comparison he was secretly making between his daughter and hers was the thought that that huge, young Viola had to be moved from the room. The idea of asking her mother to do that was infinitely embarrassing, though.

But suddenly he heard her say in a very matter-of-fact way, "What are we going to do with her? I think we must carry her to the next room with her brother."

"Carry who?" Darsh asked slowly, taken aback.

"Why, Viola of course," she said quickly, "This is the bedroom, as you can see. We should of course take Viola to the next room, don't you think?"

"Of course! Of course, we should," he said with a stupid smile, trying with affected lightness to make up for his confusion.

"I will lift her from this end," he said making his way to one end of the cradle. He lifted his end over-enthusiastically before she was ready.

"Careful! Not like that! If she wakes up, she will take a long time to go back to sleep. Don't lift the bed until I say. . . . Now!"

They carried the bed and walked with it slowly and carefully, he forward, she in reverse. All along his gaze was fixed furiously on the angelic face of the sleeping child, watching for any change in her expression that might foretell waking up. He was frightened to death that she might wake up. Not because she would take long to be brought back to sleep, but because he imagined that if she did wake up, he would lose his nerve and the whole night would be ruined.

Occasionally he lifted his eyes from the girl to the mother. He wanted to read her emotions on her face. Because what was happening was extraordinary: a mother helping a night visitor like him to move her little daughter out of the way, so they could be alone together. Totally out of the ordinary. Amazingly, he could see nothing different in her expression. All he could see was that she too was fixing her gaze on the girl's face for fear she might wake up. Perhaps that was the Austrian way of being ashamed.

Luckily, Viola did not wake up. Even though the cradle at one point hit the dining table standing in one side of the hall. When the procession arrived at the children's bedroom, she entered first and he followed cautiously. Suddenly a little voice, saturated with sleep, murmured, "Mommy!"

In a flash Darsh had put down the bed, and in one leap he was back in the hall, and then in the mother's bedroom. He only took another breath once he had shut the door and stood behind it pricking his ears for the faintest sounds. He inhaled and exhaled very slowly and calmly for the sound of his breathing not to interfere with his hearing. All this had taken place in the twinkle of eye. As if the voice that muttered "Mommy!" was that of the husband, or a gangster armed with a machine gun.

His heart beating fast with fear, Darsh kept listening. His ears picked up a faint, short conversation between the mother and one of her children. He could not tell whether it was the boy or the baby girl. But for some reason he wished it was the girl who had woken up.

It felt like ages before the handle of the door behind which he had been hiding moved to usher in the woman, barely able to suppress her laughter.

"What frightened you?" she asked.

Only then did he realize that his behavior was an indication of blatant fear, and he felt ashamed.

"Me? Frightened? Not at all. Only . . . As you know . . . I just didn't want to embarrass you in case one of the children saw me. That wouldn't have been right, of course. Don't you think?"

"Don't worry! They know nothing," she said sitting on the bed and starting to take off her shoes. "Don't be afraid now! We are alone now. Just you and me. Yes?"

He liked her words. They were the first thing she said since they met that made him feel that she really wanted him. Clearly and without any doubt. But one question still nagged him. For he was an expert on women and could swear by everything sacred that that woman was definitely a first-timer; she was neither frivolous nor adventurous. So why did she accept his advances? And even if she liked him and fell victim to his charm, why did she, a wife and mother, let him accompany her to her apartment like this? Because of all these doubts he felt reassured by her words; he felt that if he asked her any question, even concerning these very doubts, she would not be angry, and would not be too embarrassed to answer him.

He thought he should phrase his question in an innocent and touching way in order not to appear naive or intrusive in her eyes—the perfect man in his view was neither prying nor naive. Thus he stood in front of her as she was taking off her stockings, putting his hands in his pockets.

"As you have seen, I'm a direct man," he started injecting all the charm he could muster in his voice, "and there's something that's bothering me, and it will mean a lot to me if you could be frank with me."

"What is it?" she said, a little anxious.

"To put it bluntly," he said, "the question is why have you accepted me? I know that it wasn't just for a spot of good time. I know, too, that you couldn't have fallen in love with me at first sight. It is a very embarrassing question to ask, and I may seem silly in your eyes, but by God tell me why!"

She laughed bashfully. And he was sure her shyness was genuine—it was like that of women in Cairo and everywhere, complete with reddened cheeks and averted gaze.

"Not embarrassing at all," came her reply, "You are absolutely right to ask, and I don't know quite how to put in words what I want to say to you. But . . . you know . . . please don't get me wrong . . . but it is true. . . . The truth is we here in the west hear a lot about the east, its mystery, its magic, its men. I have always dreamed of that brown, eastern prince. I dreamed of him as a teenage girl, and even as a wife and mother. And when I saw you, I thought I had found him, and that it was the chance of a lifetime. Please don't think ill of me! It was the chance

51

of a lifetime, and if you hadn't got onto the tram after me, I would have got off at the next stop to come back to you. And I have lied to you: I do live with my husband but he's been away in Copenhagen for a week; he works for Scandinavian Airlines."

As she spoke, he looked down, restlessly shifting his gaze between her legs as she carried on with taking off her stockings, and his own as he stood in front of her. Her speech was anything but fluent: she hesitated, halted, or was simply indistinct.

"Have I answered your question, my eastern prince?" she asked, looking up at him after a short pause.

"Yes, you have, European woman of my dreams," said Darsh, his heart beating in that manner he knew very well when he was about to embark on something truly wonderful. So, she too had her dreams about the eastern man, virile and possessing a harem full of concubines. And he had come here especially looking for a European woman of character and rooted in civilization. What an encounter!

He expects much of her, and she must expect much of him. Where was he to begin? There must be some preliminaries. Darsh began to prepare himself, which was not easy, for much has happened and in rapid sequence, too. Nor had he had the time to absorb it all. He still did not comprehend how the woman he had met in the street an hour ago without even hope of starting a conversation with her was now at his beck and call. But comprehend or not, he must remain master of the situation. He must decide when exactly to start the preliminaries.

However, in a matter of seconds, he realized that preliminaries were altogether unnecessary. Because she did not stop at taking off her stockings, but went on to take off everything and stood in front of him stark naked.

Darsh was alarmed in the extreme. He could not remain standing. He sat down on a chair and kept staring at her naked body, all issues of preliminaries having evaporated from his mind. What exactly was the matter with this woman? Dream as she might of eastern princes— was this the best way to treat an eastern prince?

He loosened his necktie and took off his jacket to show her that he was no less daring than her. But immediately after, he heard himself ask her, "Could I use your bathroom, please?" Why the bathroom, he had no idea. At that moment he just wanted a few seconds to regain his composure and try to understand what had happened.

"The first door on your right," she said, her eyes closed.

In the bathroom he groped for the light switch until he found it and turned it on. He looked around him. It was a very small bathroom. Just like bathrooms in Egypt, as if every property builder was as stingy as the next one everywhere in the world. It was the kind of bathroom that spoke of belonging to a family living in a tiny, crowded apartment. Darsh stopped studying the bathroom and started to prepare himself to use the toilet, even though he was pretty sure he had no need to. But since he had said to her that he wanted to go to the bathroom, he ought to actually use it; as if she was going to monitor him from over there to establish whether he had said the truth or not.

Exactly opposite him as he sat on the toilet, he spotted a wash line extended between the two walls of the bathroom, like the one used by his wife in their own apartment to hang their daughter's underwear. "What use is Europe then if her people use the same objects as we do?" he thought, shrugging his shoulders. But what really attracted his attention was the fact that the line was jam-packed with children's underwear. More than twenty pieces hanging from a line not longer than two meters, and all tiny, the size of the palm of the hand. As if made to be worn by dolls. This woman must love cleanliness. Full of energy too. How could she combine working full time and looking after her home and kids?

His thoughts of approbation of the woman did not last long, because something suddenly dawned on him. It was at that moment that he realized that the woman who had brought him back to her home was really a mother. How strange! She had talked much to him about her children and he had actually carried her baby daughter with her, but he did not quite believe she was a mother until he saw this large amount of children's underwear. So, she is a mother with a home, a husband, and children. What was even more peculiar was that it was probably the first time in his life that he realized he too was a father, with a home, a wife, and a daughter, one with underwear like that which nearly rubbed against his face, and from which wafted to his nose the scent of the powder used to wash it.

He felt that he no longer wanted to use the toilet and made his way back to the bedroom. When he opened the door and entered, he no longer saw her naked. She was lying in bed (that bed made for one and a half persons) under a white sheet. Only her face and eyes were now showing. Or more accurately, there was only showing one expression, picked by Darsh as soon as he stepped into the room. An expression in which desire was mixed with resignation, and wishes with facts.

He slipped next to her in bed. He contemplated her smiling face. It was covered in tiny freckles like pinheads, visible only from close up. But he started to hear some loud ticks rising next to his ear and making him anxious: it was a small alarm clock.

"Can we take this noisy thing out of the room?" he said.

His question seemed to draw her out a little of her state of infatuation.

"I nearly forgot," she said after a short delay, "I must set it to six o'clock. I need to in order to be at the office at eight o'clock, have you forgotten?"

She set the alarm and wound it up, remarking flirtatiously, "It's now two o'clock."

When she was finished, he took the alarm from her and wrapped it in a towel to muffle its sound, then he got out of bed and placed it at the far end of the room to be finally immune from its ticking noise. Then he went back to lie next to her. But no sooner had he settled in than came the damned ticks, loud, clear, and regular. They even sounded louder than before.

Feeling nervous, he embraced her forcefully.

"You will break my back, African," she said.

African? She must call him that to provoke him into demonstrating his manhood. Or more precisely what she imagines of the virility of the eastern and African man. It was incumbent on him therefore to raise high the East's head. If he didn't, he would disappoint her, and Africa's head will be in the mire. He almost laughed out loud, imagining that the peoples of Africa had gathered together and elected him to represent their men in that contest, the contest between Africa's man and Europe's woman. But he did not laugh. He looked at that body of his, about to enter the eternal contest, and observed in it none of the characteristics of Africans. He was not black, not as tall as a coconut tree, nor was his chest covered with thick rough hair like the fiber of palm trees.

"Do you think that easterners and Africans are—I mean. . . ?" he said.

"Don't you?" she said in a moan.

Darsh embraced her tenderly. But then he remembered that he had to be 'African,' so he squeezed her between his arms and kissed her savagely. In response, she, too, embraced him and kissed him. He was a little annoyed. Why couldn't she lie back and let him do the man's job? Why couldn't she be a little shy? Shyness made a woman more feminine and a man more masculine. This over-enthusiasm of hers made her a bit like a man, in as much as it took away from his masculinity. "But wasn't this exactly what you wanted, Darsh?" he thought, "Did you not want a passionate woman who gave herself of her own will and with all her strength?"

The chimes of the clock came from the hall announcing the half hour.

"You have too many clocks," he remarked. But he was thinking it had just struck half past two; time was ticking away fast. Like her, he was an office employee, and therefore knew well the importance of punctuality. Indeed, it was not unlikely that her boss at work was like his, Dr. Nofal, the man with the disheveled hair, who had a PhD (no one knew in what), and who was obsessed with checking the attendance register personally, as if that had been the very subject of his dissertation.

For some reason Darsh cast another glance at her furtively. True, she was naked, wore a meaningless smile, and had skin that was a little too firm, and lean fingers worn out from ceaseless striking at the typewriter's keys— but she was an office employee like him.

The very next second he was furious with himself: the path his thoughts were traveling was bound to lead to catastrophe. He must concentrate and not allow himself to be distracted. He must block his ears and close his eyes. Let her be an employee or unemployed! What mattered was her being in front of him now. A naked female of flesh and blood, lying with him in the same bed behind closed doors, and found only after much toil and trouble.

He started to deal with her simply as a female. He took her hand, kissed it and put it to his cheek. He felt the coldness of metal on his skin and took her hand away: it was her wedding ring. He left that hand and picked up the other one and began to run it over his cheek. But he was thinking of her husband. He must be that man whose photo he saw in a frame above the bedside table. He moved his head until he was able to face him. He was a little on the fat side, clean shaven, no moustache, thin-haired, and smiling naively and entirely without reason.

"Are you sure your husband is not coming back tonight?" he asked.

"Of course I'm sure," she said tightening her arms around him, "he won't be back until next week. He told me that in a letter I got yesterday."

She went on talking about the letter but he was not listening. Rather, he was cursing himself. What had he got to do with her husband and his letter? Why did he keep digressing from the main 'subject'? He only had limited time and he had wasted much of it. She was more focused than he. She never asked him any questions about his person, nor did she concern herself much with his affairs, and whether he was married or widowed. All she cared for was that she was now with him in a room with a closed door.

Then silence prevailed. A heavy silence. And Darsh kept trying to dispel it, once with a movement, another time with a kiss or hug, until she relaxed again and forgot that conversation. But immediately an ingenious thought occurred to him.

"Have you got any drinks?" he asked.

"Drinks?"

"Yes. Wine? Brandy? Whisky? Or even beer?"

She knitted her brows thinking, while he succumbed to a nervous tremor, as if his fate depended on her answer. He was deeply relieved when she declared she had some brandy.

"Where?" he asked.

"There," she said as she pointed with her eyes to a small cupboard in a corner of the room.

Overjoyed, he got out of bed and opened the cupboard. He surveyed its contents until he spotted the brandy bottle at the back. There wasn't much in it. Two or three shots at most, over which floated the cork stopper. She tried to tell him where to find a glass, but he had already raised the bottle to his mouth and emptied its contents in one go, even though he could not bear the taste.

Though the brandy needed some time to reach his head, he was already feeling ecstatic. Things suddenly looked just wonderful. A beautiful woman and a night to remember to the end of life. A naked, white body tinged with reddishness. Exactly the way he wanted it. The gates of heaven are wide open to him, so what was he waiting for?

He went over to her in bed, and took her in his arms sitting up. He raised her head toward him until he could reach her mouth and started to kiss her on the lips, neck, and ears to rouse her, but she hardly needed any of that.

"My little girl!" she said suddenly.

"Listen!" she said again, before he had a chance to say anything.

From the next room came to his ears a little muffled sound with which he was well familiar, the sound of a child when it wakes from sleep without warning, crying.

"What shall I do?" she said, as if she did not really know what to do.

She got up and wrapped around her body the white bed sheet, and rushed out of the room looking like a ghost.

As soon as she shut the door behind her, he felt a kind of secret relief. He started to walk aimlessly about the room, examining its contents with the curiosity of children when left alone at home. Even her handbag; he opened it. Out of it wafted a strange smell: the fragrance of an old perfume, blended with the scents of skin, sweat, and face powder. There were also her identity card with a photo of her in which she looked like a teenager, and a key ring like any housewife's but with a different looking key which he identified as her desk drawer key at work, because it looked very much like his own Yale desk key. He went as far as to take his own key ring out of his pocket and compare the two keys, laughing. The mere resemblance of the two keys made him laugh, because by that time the heat of the brandy had gone to his head, and he started to sense that something was filling that gaping hole he had felt all the time in his chest, deep and hollow.

She came back still wrapped in the white sheet. Had she remained in that state, he would have lost no time removing it from her body. But before reaching the bed, she let it drop off her, revealing the full glory of her nakedness. He went up to her and took her in his arms with a somewhat blunted eagerness. And before anything else happened, he noticed on her face a smile about to break into laughter.

"What makes you laugh?" he asked excitedly.

"My son—he wanted to go to the bathroom."

He cursed her in his mind, wondering what was funny about something so natural. But out of politeness, he pretended to find that funny too.

"It's Alfred who usually takes care of that," she went on.

"Alfred who?"

"My husband. It's his job to get up when Tommy wakes up and take him to the toilet."

This time it was Darsh's turn to laugh out loud. She watched him convulsing with laughter.

"What's so funny?" she asked when he was finished.

"I'm more fortunate than Alfred," he replied still unable to contain his laughter.

"Why?"

He nearly replied, "Because it is not my job as a husband to take children to the toilet." But he stopped short. That was not the time. It was time to take her back to bed.

In bed Darsh tried hard to dispel all distracting thoughts from his mind. But he failed. Sometimes he lived the moment with her, but sometimes he felt that his brain had separated from him and occupied a spot near the ceiling of the room, from which it watched him and her. What an amusing sight they must be from that perspective: an eastern man and a European woman. Both married. Both with children. Both office employees. Both away from their spouses. And both ardently trying to have each other.

Everything went on in silence. Nerves tensed and trembled. Sweat beads formed on the skin and evaporated. Eyes avoided shyly to meet, but when they did meet they were shameless. Squeezes were sometimes gentle, sometimes mad. And when her child was heard crying again, his eyes commanded her, beseeched her to stay put. In preferring him over her child, he was seeking a special sign of love or desire. And when she did favor him over her child, he was again wishing that she had tried to get up for him to have stopped her by force.

Everything went on in silence, interrupted only by the stubborn ticks of the alarm clock, which persistently penetrated the towel wrapped around it, and traveled through the space of the room until they reached the openings of his ears and pounded them. On the other hand, his wristwatch was facing the wrong way, though he was constantly trying to turn it around to keep track of the time. But time was advancing at a crazy speed, heading precipitously toward six o'clock, when she had to start getting ready to go to work.

All that was beyond his endurance. And hers. They had done everything they could. Darsh had tried to shut his eyes to the entire world but her and what went on in that room. And she had tried with all her energy to help him do just that. If only she had not tried! If only she could stop trying! If only she could switch off that extended smile which sprawled over her lips and oozed out of her mouth like lipstick inexpertly applied! For after a monumental struggle Darsh was still pouring with sweat and shame. Still panting. And she still trying to help him and smiling.

"Let's smoke a cigarette!" Darsh said.

"Yes, let's!" she said.

He offered her a cigarette, which she turned around in her fingers to see the brand, then lit it, seeming to savor its quality. As for Darsh, he lit his cigarette at the filter end. Had this happened at the beginning of the night, he would have thrown it away and lit another one. But at the stage they had reached, there was no need to pretend: he snapped the filter and lit the cigarette again.

They sat up smoking.

He tried to think of her calmly. But he found that to be impossible. The more he thought of her, the more tense he became, and the deeper the empty hole he felt in his chest. Conversely, he found that the farther he drove his thoughts away from her, the more at ease he became; the more himself; the more natural; and the more in possession of his nerves, his body and his will.

It was thus that Darsh found himself thinking of his Nanusa. That being Anisa, whom he sometimes calls his Nusa, his Nanusa, or his Sansuna, to the end of the full gamut of pet names he had coined for her. Nanusa whom he had left behind in one of Ibn Khaldun Street's modest apartments. In particular he found himself thinking of her as she usually stood in the kitchen when he would come stealthily from behind and entwine his arms around her. She would be alarmed for one second but in the very next she would feel safe, and would then feel that he was the only man in the world and she the only woman suitable for him.

For a fleeting moment Darsh thought he was dreaming. But he actually had a woman in his arms, his eyes closed. He was so worried that if the woman moved, Nusa's image would fade away, he commanded her not to move. He muttered a few words, hardly audible, asking her to switch off the light.

He saw nothing. Because he kept his eyes closed. He only heard the flick of the light switch above the bed. And even after he was assured that darkness had prevailed in the room, he kept his eyes closed. He did not want to see anything. He only saw his bed and his Nusa, and only heard her tender whisperings to him, and the distant voices of street peddlers crying their goods in Ibn Khaldun Street.

He sighed in relief as he was tying his shoelaces. He had already put on all his clothes, and all he had left to do was to run the comb through his hair and leave the room and the whole apartment. All he was thinking of at that moment was how to get back to his hotel. It was still only a little past five o'clock and he did not have a clue how at such an early hour and from so far-flung a suburb to reach downtown Vienna where his Hotel Victoria was situated. He asked her and she mentioned a taxi stand at the bottom of the street.

He looked at her as she spoke. For the first time he felt he had power over her: he had transcended the crisis and performed exceedingly well. She looked calm, relaxed, and content, and that exaggerated smile had totally disappeared from her face. He nearly censured her in his mind for the way she felt. But he had finished with her: she did not matter to him any more.

Having combed his hair and felt in his pockets for his cigarette packet and key ring, it was time to leave and put an end to the night. In fact, it had actually ended as the nascent morning light was making its way into the room through the window blinds. But he did not understand why he stood there awkwardly, neither staying nor leaving. He had accomplished all he had set out to do, even if after considerable difficulty, so why all this hesitation? What did he want? He had no idea. But something was bothering him. No, it wasn't disappointment. Nor a prick of conscience. It was something else.

Throughout the night he was with Nusa, his wife. He was with her, body and soul. With all his being. And if it weren't for that, he wouldn't have functioned. He wouldn't have lived up to the reputation of the African man. And that woman still lying in bed, wallowing in her sense of satisfaction—that woman thought he had been with her. But, no, he hadn't. As for Nusa, she might think, if she knew, that he had been unfaithful to her, but what nonsense! It was nothing of the sort. He had been all the time with her, Nusa.

They were tiny miniscule thoughts that he could not isolate and pin down. Nonetheless they kept assaulting him, dealing thin, sharp, and painful pricks to his consciousness. Maybe that was why he said what he had finally said to the woman. It had occurred to him to say to her that when they were making love, he had been with his wife, not with her. At first he rejected the thought utterly. But he had grown careless and felt he could behave toward her in whatever manner he wanted, that he could say to her whatever struck his mind, and do with her whatever he liked. Besides, he was never going to see her again, nor she him. That was their last encounter in life, so why shouldn't he tell her the truth? What did it matter if she was angry? If she cried? As long as what he said was right. Was true. And as long as it was going to relieve his conscience.

He was on the point of saying it. But it seemed he lost heart at the last moment. What came out of his mouth were different words. He asked her to give him her telephone number and promised to call her in the evening. Though he had no intention whatsoever to do so.

Her eyes remained shut as she dictated the number. But when she was finished and there was no movement in the room to indicate his departure, and no words of leave-taking were heard, she opened her eyes and saw him still standing strangely there. It was then that that expansive smile returned to her face. He realized that she too felt awkward and unable to ask him why he stood there when everything called for him to go.

As soon as he saw that smile again, all hesitation was gone and he was about to tell her the truth he had been withholding until then. But to his surprise, her smile began to expand further and further until it engulfed her entire face before turning into an audible laugh, a laugh that rang strange and cold at that early hour of the morning. He asked her what made her laugh.

"It's embarrassing," she said.

"Just tell me!" he said sharply.

"It's very embarrassing."

"Please," he now pleaded fearing his sharpness might be counterproductive, "I think we now are past embarrassment. Do tell me!"

But she did not answer. She opened her eyes and turned in bed toward her husband's photo standing on the bedside table. She stared at the picture deliberately before stretching her naked arm from under the bed sheet and picking it up, drawing it close to her face. It was at that point that she spoke.

"Do you know that I've been with him?" she said.

"With whom?"

"Alfred."

"When?"

"All the time I was with you." And again she laughed. The same laugh with which she had started the conversation.

She kept holding the picture in her hand, her face hidden by it from his view. He could only see her arm now, which in the mixture of electric and dawn light appeared pale and covered in light, blonde hair.

She kissed him. She kissed Alfred, her husband in the picture before returning it to its place.

"I had no idea he was my African man, for whom I have been searching," she said in a sleepy murmur as she turned in bed to face the wall, giving her back to Darsh: he no longer mattered to her either. Life turned black in Darsh's eyes, and he felt his head sizzling. Suddenly he turned on his heels and left the apartment. He felt furious at his humiliation.

The world outside was celebrating sunrise. Everything was quiet and still, but preparing to receive the new day. Everything was new. The day was new. The people were new. Even the air was new, as yet un-breathed by anyone. The streets were still deserted, and the gray light of early morning was advancing on the street lamps, fast outshining their luster, making them look like fruit out of season.

Before turning around the last block, Darsh heard in the distance the bell of an alarm clock going off in muffled persistence. No doubt it was hers. And no doubt she was struggling now to shed off sleeplessness, tiredness, and the warmth of the bed to go to work and rejoin her world.

Darsh no longer felt angry with her. Not even with himself. All he felt at that moment was a strange sweeping nostalgia for his home and his family and the great wide world from which he had come.

NEW YORK 80

1

HE: Excuse me, madam—by the way, is this the right way to speak to women? Or should I say, ma'am?

She looks at him, surprised and a little disapproving.

SHE: You can say it either way—why not? It's a very common form of address here.

HE: Madam . . . it's clear that you are . . . that you . . .

SHE: Yes, yes. To save your time and mine. I'm a call girl—do you know what that means? To save even more time, I'm what people call a prostitute.

Although her answer did not take him by surprise, he found her manner quick and aggressive. His brain worked at the speed of lightning: he repeated the question and answer to himself several times, not to make sure, but to absorb it. When he finished censuring himself for his shyness and regained control of himself, he looked up and faced her.

HE *(internal monologue)*: A prostitute? Why is everything here called by its name? Have they no shame? We are more polite. Call it pretense, call it hypocrisy—still it is more decent than the plain truth and the words that reflect it with precision. Prostitute! The word will be awful in any language. Even in French. Even Sartre's *La Putain respectueuse*: "The Respectable Prostitute"! *(A savage torrent of taboos and tableaus sweeps his consciousness, like New York's rain.)*

But there is truth. And truth must be said. This lady of his does not look like a prostitute in any manner. She wears fashionable prescription glasses. Oh, how he worships women in glasses! The eyes of those wearing them are usually clear, precisely defined, and they reveal their most guarded inclinations, especially toward men. Prostitute! She must be new to the job. As if she only started yesterday. What's certain, however, is that this girl posesses a magnetic force—nothing to do with her trade—which attracts her to the male sex, even before they are attracted to her.

HE *(to her)*: Madam! Or as you say in American, Ma'am! I want to make something very clear from the start. I arrived here before you, and I noticed that when you arrived, you searched the place with your eyes, and though most places were empty, you chose the sofa on which I was sitting to come and sit on the other end. I have also noticed that three men, one after the other, had left their seats at the bar to come make advances to you. Yes, I was watching you deliberately.

Indeed, I took pity on you, and I thanked God I wasn't created a female who chose to be a call girl. Especially as the last man was so obese and fit for nothing but to be slapped on the back of his neck. I even noticed how he was trying to seduce you by mentioning the name of the fearsome international corporation he works for.

SHE *(interrupting)*: He was smelly, too.

HE: This is deplorable and disgusting. But you are a free woman, and you have chosen to put yourself up for sale to men. You are free. But your freedom must stop here. I have also noticed that you rejected those men with their fat wallets because you had your eye on me: you kept looking furtively in my direction. But I want to be as frank with you as I can. I utterly despise your kind. I cannot imagine a woman selling her body no matter how much she needed money. And you don't look like you're starving. On the contrary, I can see around your finger a platinum ring worth no less than a thousand dollars. I hate your kind. It disgusts me. It makes me want to throw up looking at women like you. And so that you may know, I'm not waiting for anybody, neither man nor woman. But I am very tired and I find this sofa comfortable and have no intention of changing my place.

(What a strange woman! She listens without getting angry. It's like I was talking to someone else. Talk some more then!)

73

HE *(continuing)*: I despise your kind to a point beyond the imagination of someone like you, insensitive even to insults. As I have already told you, I know that you declined customers because you have your eyes on me—I don't know why. But let me tell you that I'd sooner sleep with a gorilla than with you: it's a matter of principle. You and the like of you, I consider enemies. And if I were a natural criminal, I would kill your kind. I shall never be your customer. Please leave! Find yourself another client! I want to be honest even with someone like you.

She turned fully in his direction. He was astounded when he saw her face at close quarters. In his experience, prostitutes usually smear their faces with exaggerated makeup, while their hair is often pastiche or dressed in a showy manner. In Cairo or any other capital he would recognize them from their appearance a mile away. By contrast this woman sitting near him wore minimal makeup; her face was almost natural. Her round spectacles are very feminine but tastefully so. If you met her somewhere else, you would think her the deputy head of public relations at the United Nations (deputy head, not head, because she must be only between twenty-five and thirty years old). No inviting smiles. No overt show of interest. Dignified without affectation. Respectable, like someone who took her job seriously. On her face was the ghost of a purple smile matching elegantly her non-gloss lipstick.

SHE: Do I understand that you want me to leave my place?
HE: Not at all. I haven't said that.
SHE: Why don't you leave my sofa, then?
HE: This isn't *your* sofa. Nor mine. It belongs to the café, and I have no intention of moving.
SHE: It's all about your not liking prostitutes then?
HE: Neither prostitutes nor semi-prostitutes. Not even a woman who would make love in return for a meal out or a present. It is abhorrent. It is beneath animals.

He realized that she was unleashing her charm on him. No, she couldn't be a beginner in her profession. Not with that sleight of hand. In the very next thread of conversation, she could gain the upper hand. What was he going to do? This was the very first time in his life to sit so close to a prostitute, let alone have a conversation with her. Back in his country and in his many travels, he had encountered many of her kind, those who did it as a pastime, and those who did it for money. But they were all shy and sensitive: no sooner would he turn his face away or show annoyance than they would leave him alone. They would use their hidden antennae to look for another customer, or leave the place entirely. But this one was of a new type. She was enormously self-confident. She knows no shame and can adjust her approach as needed. Maybe she had time on her hands. Or—if he were to flatter himself—she wanted him in particular.

SHE: Tell me truthfully why you don't like prostitutes.

HE: Because I believe that love—even physical love—cannot be bought for money.

She breaks out laughing. A laugh not even like that of the women of the classy Gezira Club in Cairo. Actually more conservative. But from the heart.

HE *(repeats his sentence verbatim)*: Because I believe that love—even physical love—cannot be bought for money.

She laughs again. The sarcasm in her laughter now clearer, as if he were a buffoon. Or at least someone uttering sheer nonsense.

HE *(in Arabic)*: I beg your pardon?
SHE: What? What did you say?
HE *(again in Arabic)*: I beg your pardon?
SHE: What language is this?
HE: Some language.
SHE: Greek?
HE: No.
SHE: Polish?
HE: No.
SHE: What country do you come from?

He doesn't want to get carried away. She is turning on more charm and he feels weakened. He cannot allow this to happen. This is a woman who sells a woman's most valuable possession for money. She treats her body as if it were a sack of potatoes or a bunch of radishes. Scorn welled up in him until it reached his throat. Even her perfumed scent, and his, turned into something like the scents of meat and vegetable markets in Paris, the stomach of Paris. Or like the scents of the animal-hide market at the back of the Alexandria port.

HE: I beg your pardon?
SHE: What country are you from?

Answer her roughly, stupid man, to make her go!

HE: I'm from somewhere in the world.
SHE: And what do you do for a living?
HE: Some job.
SHE: What do you mean some job? Every person must have a job—what's yours?
HE: A job of the kind that those men in front of you in the bar have—those clean-shaven, well-groomed men.
SHE: Are you a businessman?
HE: I'm a man without business.
SHE: Why are you trying to be mysterious?
HE: Because I don't trust you.
SHE: Even in telling me what kind of job you do?
HE: Yes, even that.

She turned fully toward him. O God have mercy! She was the most beautiful female. And not only at this bar.

It had been a long time since he had seen a young woman of such beauty, let alone sit next to one, and talk and be rude to her. It wasn't that she had green eyes, golden hair, and lips like Brigitte Bardot's: she had skin the color of reddish wheat. As for her features, they were shaped by a consciousness that missed nothing. The kind of beauty that God formed in a moment of *bien-être* and then left for her to fine-tune with her extraordinary intelligence. She added magnetism to it, such that once your eyes fell on her, they would remain fixed on her. A young woman with whom he could only fall in love. Indeed, the sort of woman for whom he would drop his most cherished commitments. For her and the likes of her, careers are abandoned and men wasted.

But she sells her body. This precious work of art is up for sale.

Suddenly he is seized by commercial curiosity, like Egyptian housewives walking around Oxford Street in London: they want to know the price at once, though the last thing they are thinking of is buying.

HE: How much are you?

SHE: For a quickie? One hour? A whole night? A month?

HE *(in Arabic)*: Unbelievable bitch!

SHE: You speak English fluently—so why this strange language? Are you afraid to confront me, you, you— what shall I call you?—the man who cannot bear the idea of a woman offering him herself so clearly, frankly, and openly.

HE: I was calling you names. *(He says this with real difficulty.)*

SHE *(simply and spontaneously)*: What kind? In New York, the most common word of abuse is 'bullshit,' onward to all types of body discharges, apertures, and protrusions.

HE: *(carrying on with her list)*: And the bodies of mothers, fathers, and siblings.

SHE: I don't understand you.

HE *(aggressively)*: And is 'bullshit' understandable? Not all terms of abuse are possible to understand. Which is fine, because the less understood, the more insulting.

SHE: Did you really call me names?

HE: Yes, by way of expressing shock.

He decided not to say anything further, however hard she tried to drag him into conversation. He turned his gaze to the bar. There was no way of telling whether the other women around were prostitutes or not. (There was no longer any difference in this crowded place.) He was filled with scorn for women, present and absent, beautiful and ugly. They all wore one or another of their plentiful masks. She fixed her stare on him, half-wearing her professional smile.

SHE: You were asking about my price.

He was perplexed. Should he respond and reopen the door for conversation ? A nagging curiosity was pecking at the veneer of his willpower, now brittle like the shell of a fresh egg. He remained silent.

She smiled. A 'businesslike' smile that she soon realized was in excess of what the situation required. Despite the dim lighting, he glimpsed in her eyes something very delicate, very fragile, that had to do with him.

The headwaiter approached her, dressed in an elegant tuxedo worthy of Sir Miles Lampson, the last British High Commissioner in Egypt, but more handsome, leaner, and with a straighter back. He looked serious, with a stony face, like a chief judge in the court of cassation. He thought he was approaching her to ask her to leave the place as his counterparts would have done back home. But that was not the case: he had noticed a man with silver hair—more beautiful than Omar Sharif's—whisper something to him from his stool at the far end of the bar. He could only see the back of his head, having turned to continue his conversation with a corpulent man of brown complexion and an oval-shaped body who wore an Asian head covering.

The regally mannered waiter bent over her and whispered a few words. She listened and smiled, then shook her head slowly, glancing in the direction of the fat customer. It was a polite rejection of his invitation.

(It was clear that she had made her choice and settled on him. But you will be disappointed, my respectable prostitute.)

Now she looked toward him without a smile.
SHE: You were asking about my price?

His defenses broke down, clearing the way to the triumph of curiosity. He wanted to know the price of the prostitute sitting in a New York café and looking more decent and respectable, nay more beautiful and attractive, than Jacqueline Kennedy. It was that kind of beauty which unleashed in him a wolfish Casanova, and hurled him into a region without gravity.

HE: Yes, how much are you?

SHE: For a quickie, a hundred dollars; for a whole night, three hundred dollars.

HE: And for a whole month?

SHE: If you like me, three thousand dollars. This is a discounted price, as you can see. It works out at a hundred dollars per night.

HE: And if I don't like you?

SHE: I thought I was talking to a smart man—if you don't like me for one night, why would you be interested in a whole month?

One droplet of cold sweat formed at the nape of his neck. He was facing a highly intelligent woman. This is not how prostitutes talk. The first time he encountered them he was still a university student. His flatmate was fond of them, like his father. In fact, he and his father sometimes took turns with them. Their flat became famous among the street girls of Qasr al-Aini, Munira, and as far away as Madbah. Girls who remained until late at night without clients used to be short, thin, and shoddily dressed, and most, as he used to think, suffered from VD. He once treated one for scabies, causing the flat to smell of sulphur for days. They used to come, three or four of them, and sometimes as many as five, to sleep on the cold, tiled floor of the hallway without covers. They found that a better shelter than the street and standing under lamp posts to solicit customers. No sooner had they rested their heads on the floor than they fell asleep. One of them used to wake up in alarm and rouse everyone else, crying from a frightful nightmare. In a moment of terror she explained to them that the cause was her uncle who raised her and who used to beat her and then rape her. But why the crying and the hysteria? Because she used to go to sleep having been beaten up and raped, now going to sleep normally brought her nightmares, she would tell them, nightmares of dying. The beating made her feel alive, and rape made her live in anticipation of another night.

On one occasion, Awad, his flatmate, rummaged in the purse of one of them out of curiosity—none had a handbag except Tahiya. He found in it five piasters, a blue amulet, a few hairpins, and a very old letter from a brother of hers containing nothing but greetings. What was really puzzling was a little bottle full of concentrated tincture of iodine. At first he thought she used it for cleansing herself after 'work.' But iodine tincture at that strength is caustic so that couldn't be. In the morning he confessed to his prying and asked her about the bottle.

"Oh, that's to drink, if I'm caught," she said casually.

"If who caught you?"

"The vice police."

"But why? They will only hold you for a few days— nothing to commit suicide for."

"Most of us carry bottles like this," she said. "The woman who taught me the profession told me to carry one, just in case."

"To kill yourself?"

"So?"

"To die?"

"I lead a dog's life. And my clients also lead a dog's life."

"So why are you still living? Why haven't you drunk it until now?"

"Life is dear. This is meant as the last resort."

"Have you ever used it?"

"No, but one of my friends did."

"Did she live?"

"She's still in the hospital," she said, "and anyway, what's the fuss about? One of two things will happen. If cornered, I drink it and die and I'm relieved of walking the streets, sleeping on the floor, and being burned with cigarette butts to satisfy kinky clients. If I don't die, they will take me to the hospital—the police have to do that even if they don't care. As for the stomach pump and its horrors that they talk about—well, that's my life: tubes, insertions, fluids, and washes; it's all the same. What really matters is to spend a few days in the hospital with free food, drink, and sleep, and without the smell of men."

"But you will come out again for the street dogs."

"True, but while I'm in the hospital, I will get another bottle of concentrated tincture of iodine."

"Who gives it to you?"

"A male nurse."

"For free?"

"Nothing is for free," she says, "five minutes with him in one of the many toilets of Qasr al-Aini Hospital."

SHE: You look like a very smart man. I've never met anyone with your intuition. But sometimes you say things . . . er . . . things that do not do justice to your intelligence. You must be a scientist? Maybe a professor? No, you are too young to be a professor. Perhaps a stage director? I was going to say an actor, but there was absolutely no acting in the way you behave toward me. Who are you exactly? From which country? And what is your job?

She is adamant to drag him in.

HE: And what does it matter to you, madam, who I am or what I do? I'm not and will not be a client of yours—so what use is it to you to know who I am?

SHE: Because we are talking to each other. We've been talking for a whole half hour. And now you know who I am, but I don't know who you are, and this is . . . this is . . .

HE: Impolite?

SHE: No, not that. There's a more suitable word: fear. You are afraid of me. Afraid to the core. Your knees are shaking with fear of me—what are you afraid of?

HE: Concentrated iodine tincture.

SHE: Concentrated iodine tincture?

HE: Yes, in your prostitute's bag of tricks.

SHE: There are no liquids in my bag except for my perfume, the world's best. *(She opens her handbag, takes out the
bottle, and without warning holds his hand and pours a drop on
the back of it.)* Smell!

His skin went on fire. He nearly let out a cry. Extreme
pain showed on his face.

SHE: Smell it! It's the greatest perfume ever made by
Sonia Magdalena. Smell!

What hit his nose was the armpit smell of a woman not
used to cleanliness. Yet, beyond the circle of the drop on
his skin, the atmosphere was redolent with an intoxicating
fragrance that wafted in the bar, rendering the scents of
booze, the *fruits de mer*, and the smoke of cigarettes and
cigars into something like the incense of an Indian temple,
where only monks were allowed; monks who blended in
their prayers the age-old clerical scents with the scents of
a modernity that landed mankind on the moon. But when
he went back to the spot on his skin, the very source of all
those thoughts, all he could smell was the scent of a stale
armpit. His features contracted and he blocked his nostrils. He felt his stomach coming up into his throat.

She stared at him while inhaling the scents of the
place. She put a drop of the perfume on the back of her

85

hand and surrendered to the titillating fragrance infiltrating her butterfly nostrils. Her face, too, turned into ether before the expression on his face hurled her down to earth from her ecstatic state.

SHE: This is the most expensive perfume on earth, don't you know that?
HE: Yes, I know.
SHE: Do you know how much it costs?
HE: Yes, I do.
SHE: How much?
HE: Five minutes in a toilet of Qasr al-Aini Hospital.

2

SHE: You have a hangup, my dear. A serious hangup. Do you know why you hate so much the idea of making love with a prostitute?

To talk to someone and continue to do so, even if you hate him or her, means that you get to know the person despite your intentions. And this familiarity tends to diminish the antagonism, or at least domesticate it. He knows why he hates prostitutes and has no need to know more.

HE: Because I hold as sacred the human body and the human soul.

SHE: What do you mean "holding as sacred the human body"? Or did you mean humankind?

HE *(to himself)*: You slut! Stop being so precise. You are not Bertrand Russell, nor the director of the language academy. Yes, it's because I hold humankind sacred, and therefore sex, and the mind, and human feelings. I'm not a bull, and a woman isn't a cow; I'm not a stray dog and a woman isn't a bitch in heat.

HE *(to her)*: Did you get what I haven't uttered?

SHE: You are only half an intellectual. And I now know three things about you. First, you are a writer. Second, you are still a child emotionally and mentally. Third, the true reason for your fear of me seems to be that you think I'm too expensive.

He: Aha! You want to play your favorite game: to go on the offensive in order to put me on the defensive.

SHE: No. What I want is to prove to you that the prostitute that I am understands human nature far better than you do with all your experience, your studies, and your talent.

HE: You! The woman who makes a business of selling her body!

He said those words with disgust. As if he could see her living flesh on offer in a modern supermarket wrapped in cling film with a price tag: $100 an hour or $300 a night.

SHE: Is that how I would be seen in your country? What is your country? Your features are neither eastern nor western, but they have touched something in me.

HE: I shall never tell you who I am or what I do. We have talked longer than we should but I must admit I'm not disinclined to go on, despite being against it in principle.

SHE: Why you want to go on is because you feel our conversation is going to lead you to knowing exactly who you are.

HE: I'm a human being of this world and this age.

SHE: You are the product of your mother, your father, your family, and your society. *And* the arrest of your emotional growth.

Could he be dreaming? A prostitute speaking with such knowledge and such logic? Even specialist terminology! She is more than just educated. More than a psychologist. This is unbelievable.

HE *(like one insulted)*: You say my emotional growth has been arrested?
SHE: Yes. You are a crippled man.

He had learned from Euro-American societies—nay, perhaps it was a human instinct—that unless you attack, you will be attacked, and that if your attack is intense and eloquent, your cause will win. We acquired our excessive politeness and gentle approach from ages of speaking quietly: too softly for us to hear each other for fear of the tyrants who ruled us overhearing us. In truth, there was no denying that he was angered by her reference to the "arrest of his emotional growth."

HE: Do I look like a dwarf to you?
SHE: You are a tall man, and you have tough muscles—I know that because I happen to have touched your thigh unintentionally. Your muscles have escaped the effects of the soft life I think you now lead. All that's manly and mature in you are your muscles.

HE: I'm a writer, you . . .

The hesitation here means that he now doubted the reality of the name he was about to call her.

SHE: Say it! It's nothing that I'm ashamed of. Everyone here knows I'm a prostitute. That's how I introduce myself. And why should I be ashamed? I am actually a prostitute—no one should be ashamed of their profession.

HE: But your profession is a shameful one. A thief, for instance, doesn't take pride in his job to the extent that he goes about introducing himself as a thief.

SHE: That's because 'thief' is not a label he gives himself, but what other people call him. And remember, a thief steals what he doesn't own, but I offer what is mine. In fact, people steal from me and not the other way around. It's just another word for businessman— I'm a businesswoman in my own way. You too are a 'businessman.'

Thoughts poured over him like torrential rain. But suddenly there was the mightiest explosion he has ever heard in his life. He thought Earth had collided with another planet gone astray in space, but it was only one of those thunderstorms familiar in New York and the east coast. But it was not familiar to him. Thunder pounded his ears ruthlessly. And there was lightening too as he had never seen except in movies. Amid the thunder and the lightening he stood stripped of all his haloes in front of a woman whose job it is to strip for men. And yet there she was in front of him fully clothed while he shuddered with cold and fear. In his own country he only had to utter his name for everyone to bow in humility before his ideas and pronouncements. Over decades he had built himself a fort of his intellect, his personality, his intelligence, and his talent. He used to feel humbled when others prostrated before his might. But when this becomes the pattern, it turns into absolute power, into arrogance. And in every man, as in him, there is a tyrant awaiting the opportunity to rise unopposed.

This is a woman who hardly knows him, but understands him fully. Their conversation has turned into a trial in which he stands accused. Whenever he talks, words spring from a source inside him that he knows well; they arrive spontaneously and truthfully. This time too, his words in response to her candidness, her objectivity, her brazenness—they come as usual, spontaneous and true. But the source inside him—the source of whose purity and genuineness he had always been sure—his faith in it is now beginning to falter. His words now are a mixture of truth and lies. He no longer understands. His confusion is threatening to engulf him. Let him erase this woman from existence! At least his own existence. Let this entire place be razed to the ground.

HE *(in a hoarse voice, as if on the verge of committing murder)*:
   Listen, Professor . . .

SHE: Yes, my student? *(Followed by a trailing laugh.)*

HE: Stop this frivolity that has wasted my time and yours! I came to this place, tired, after a long hard day, looking for nothing but a sandwich and some ginger ale. And I've told you many times that I'm not going to be your client, nor a client of anyone like you. Even if you turned out to be some former queen or royal daughter or something. Even if you were to commit suicide if I didn't go with you. Listen! I have no doubt that you've wasted my time, but I'm not sure I've wasted yours. And yet because of this possibility, I'm going to offer you a drink to make up for your time.

SHE: You don't have to do that. I decline. I haven't been doing 'business' with you. I've only been having a friendly conversation with you. There's no charge for that.

HE: You mean to tell me there's still some generosity in America? What's upset me in your talk is that it has proved to me a kind of terrible degeneration. Not just in your civilization as a whole, but in the most important element in it, indeed in any civilization: womankind. You are rotten spiritually, intellectually, and philosophically. And what shocks me is that you can find clients among men; men who grew up in a society that's supposed to be civilized; that's supposed to have transcended the primitive, commercial relationship between man and woman. How can a man living in the most advanced country in the world in the second half of the twentieth century find it acceptable to obtain a woman, or at least the body of a woman, for a few dollars that he pays her in return for stripping herself inside out for him? A civilization that can land on the moon through its lofty scientific knowledge, while still practicing white slavery, makes me sick. I feel sick at a woman like you—and you are but one of many—intelligent, educated, widely read *and* beautiful, more beautiful than movie stars, doing a job that any deranged woman can do; a job in which all you have to do is . . . you know of course what I mean. How can a woman like you, so delicate and so sensitive—how can you let a man lie on top of you with his weight, with his paunch, with his sweat and stickiness, with the drunken smell of his breath in return for . . . . In return for what? No amount of money is worth a human being letting her soul plummet to such a stinking gutter.

You speak logically, intelligently, like an experienced woman. But these are trophies you have collected from the folds of stained bed linen. From the bruises and cuts of your body and soul. Yours is the intelligence of a woman who has sold her soul in return for a rationale with which to smother what is left of her human essence. When I started talking to you, I was disgusted at you. Now I'm disgusted at myself. Disgusted that I have wasted so much time with a person so impeccably clean on the outside, but so ridden with disease inside. The dirtiest thing is not for a human being to appear dirty from outside; in fact, inner purity may make the soul so radiant that external stains may be forgiven.

SHE: Listen! I will spend the whole night with you for just a hundred dollars.

Without replying, his face frozen in a horrifyingly cruel expression, he started to collect his things. He felt sick at the entire human race: its civilization, industry, arts, and philosophers and moralists—for what use were they? She seems to have read them all and yet none of them has managed to convince her that human beings were something else other than spurts of ejaculate and receptacles for it. Maybe none of them was genuine enough to convince her.

HE: First of all, I only have twenty dollars. Second, if I had twenty thousand or twenty million dollars, and you asked for just one for a night, I would rather spend it on polishing my shoes. At least I will be cleaning something.

SHE: Listen, let's talk business! Just try! For you, I will charge only twenty dollars, on condition that if you enjoyed it, you give me a hundred.

HE: You must be really deranged. Can't you understand that a purely physical relation can give no pleasure for someone like me?

SHE: This is because you are not yet mature enough to enjoy it. I will bring you to maturity.

HE: Not yet mature enough? It's only a teenager that can enjoy that purely physical thing. But a man at the height of his emotional development cannot find pleasure in a physical experience devoid of reciprocal feeling.

SHE: That's because, as I told you, you have not matured yet. Mutual feelings and what you call love before physical contact—all these are symptoms of immaturity of man or woman. True maturity lies in the enjoyment of the sexual act without prerequisites.

HE: Listen, Professor. These views of yours—keep them to yourself! I am confirmed in my view that you are nothing but a professional sex worker, without feeling, cut off from humanity.

SHE: Allow me . . .

HE: No, please. I don't want to listen to you any more. It's true I have certain principles, but I am a fair man. And I know you could have been making money from another man in the time you spent talking to me. Take my twenty dollars, which is extremely generous of me, considering what I think of you and the way you've wasted my time. Here is the twenty! And I hope we never meet again.

3

I n his hotel there were instructions to lock your room
door well and not to answer to visitors unless there was
a call from reception first. Also, if you do open the
door, not to unfasten the security chain until you could
identify the visitor through the gap. There was nothing of
all that in the sixties. It was in the seventies and eighties
with the rise in violence and assaults, even on hotel
guests, that all these security instructions appeared.

There's a knock on his door.

HE: Who's there?

A VOICE: It's me.

HE: Who are you?

THE VOICE: I'm the night manager of the hotel.

HE: But this is a woman's voice.

THE VOICE: Yes, but I am the night manager.

HE: No, madam manager. It's you. No need for
stupid tricks. I'm ready for bed, and I'm tired of
being chased. If you don't leave me alone, I will
call the real manager. I will call security, or even
the police.

SHE: Please, I have not come as a prostitute. I've come with a message. You are an important man; it's vital that I persuade you of my message. I'm talking to— I'm begging—the artist in you.

HE: I'm no artist. I'm just an angry animal now. Beware of my anger!

SHE: Beware *you* of my appreciation! As I've just told you, I'm a woman with a message. And my message matters more to me than my personal dignity.

HE: Please! My patience is running out. And whatever your message is, it doesn't concern me.

SHE: But it does. Very much.

HE: My patience has run out—I'm warning you again.

SHE: Rather, it's your courage that's run out. Are you afraid of a woman? With a message?

HE: If it's a woman whose message is to sell her body, then yes, that's something to be afraid of.

SHE: But that's not what I am. My mission is to dress the wounds of men: I'm a doctor.

HE: You mean a veterinarian?

SHE: No. I'm a doctor and psychotherapist. Please! Here is my identity card—read it quickly! There are people coming. I don't want any problems, neither for you, nor for me.

She pushes the card under the door. It couldn't be fake. It shows her photo in color. Central Park Hospital. Pamela Graham. Psychotherapist. The hospital is one of New York's, actually America's, biggest hospitals. The card is genuine. It is the woman from the café. Everything is turned upside down now. The hint of impropriety in her face now acquired an intellectual depth. His deep scorn for her now gave way to bewilderment, which gushed up from his soul like a hot-water jet long suppressed underground.

The first thought that struck him was that their conversation earlier in the night was not accidental; that everything was prearranged. As a man from the 'third world' in this developed society (developed even in its crimes) he lived in a state of utmost suspicion. He was targeted then. Maybe she was specifically chosen to assassinate him. They are clever enough to know that half an Oriental man's mind would be reduced to droolery by the mere fact that she was a woman, and the other half at the merest touch on his skin by her little finger.

As for the notion that being a woman would make her an unlikely murderer, that was a red herring, because in this brutal, advanced society, women learned brutality from men. Sometimes they actually fed brutality to men.

He laughs suddenly. Part genuinely from the heart; part nervously to conceal his fear.

HE *(to himself)*: But why would anyone think of killing me? And why would they use a woman psychotherapist disguised as a whore (or maybe a whore disguised as psychotherapist?) to execute me? Surely there must be an easier way? But again why would they want to kill me in the first place? And who are those who care to kill me? Surely theft couldn't be the reason.

All he has in his possession now is seven dollars and some coins, in addition to traveler's checks only cashable by himself. He really was a man coming from the third world with all its fears and misgivings. He had every right to feel that way toward a 'first-world' developed country, whose foremost mark of development was the ease with which crimes were committed in it, despite all security precautions and all the wailing sirens of police cars, ambulances, and fire engines. The more wailing sirens, the more muggers, guns, and knives behind them, while the ordinary person, especially foreigners, can only feel tense, drawn as they are between the futilely wailing sirens, on the one hand, and the crimes silently and anonymously committed, on the other. What a mockery! The police advertise themselves through wailing patrol cars, while criminals lie in wait before they leap out of nowhere. Or sometimes a criminal might turn up disguised. With an identity card. As a doctor. Or by way of excessive disguise, as a psychotherapist.

One moment, a fraction of a moment, an interlude sharp as a razor, made the difference between what he is now and the little child that the Arabic language teacher used to smack on his shaven head, saying "Sit down, sickly child!"; the child whose drawings the art teacher used to pin up in the classroom for a whole month for teachers and pupils (and even Ragab, the school janitor) to scoff at their ugliness; the child whose stepmother was so certain of his failure, she had vowed to shave her head if he passed his exams. One moment made the difference for that child, that seedling that grew in terror of the high leafy trees, seeking safety in hiding underground, until in a daring moment, he conquered his shyness and hesitancy and peeped out of earth still trembling with fear of insects, worms, and cattle egrets; that child/seedling which could have been plucked out and met an early death like so many before it who lost their lives while digging the Suez Canal, or in some war to which they would have been driven without a word of explanation, or just running after a bus. No better than seedlings, or little blades of grass, was the child's generation and many before it. Just pastureland for the bulls, for cattle and sheep, for fattened turkeys.

And here he was! All alone. With a woman like that from an advanced world civilization, taking pride in being a whore. Without an iota of shame or guilt. It was he who felt ashamed for her. For her lack of embarrassment of her profession, of what she did with him, and of doing what she did while being a psychotherapist. In his country, all this was improper. Shameful. Brazen.

But every rule has an exception. And he, who began as a grass seedling in the ground, has shown daring by pushing aside the specks of earth and raising his head above ground. He was not intimidated by the towering trees but climbed over their roots and trunks. Then he became independent with his own roots deeply stuck in the ground. And before long he became taller than camphor trees, straighter and with leaves more prickly than the needles of pine trees.

But during the journey from the belly of the earth to the surface, to the expansive horizon, to dominance over the woods, he was stricken with diseases and ailments. The huge trunks nearly smothered him. And when he escaped those, he was nearly done in by parasitical plants. But he vanquished all and sundry. He cracked the earth open and split the air, rising to become the highest mast of the largest ship. He crossed seas; he fought battles; he freed captives and captured women—from royalty and slave girls alike—and made of them his harem. With extraordinary power latent in him he did all that. Single-handedly he did all that. Would he now be afraid of a woman?

But he was actually afraid. For the first time he was afraid. Whatever she was: a prostitute carrying a doctor's identity, or a doctor with a vice-squad officer's identity— he was afraid. Because this time they did not come for him with his match, but with his opposite. His anti-person.

This opposite of his engulfed him. Engulfed the Oriental man inside him. The Oriental man smitten with pants. Long pants. Short pants. Hot pants. The Oriental man smitten with the swimsuit on a white female with a body of ingenious measurements. The Oriental man smitten with a white female on roller skates swaying like a ballerina down Fifth Avenue. Sixth Avenue. Third Avenue. Swinging right and left. Rocking to music only she could hear from her noise-reduction earphones, while passersby could only listen to it through the movements of her soft malleable figure. If you saw her while walking, you would stop; while stopping, you would start walking: the swaying body turned into red, amber, and green traffic lights. She halted traffic or made it flow. She turned heads and made their hair stand on end. Pity the eyes that saw her legs come apart, widening the gap between them, before they narrowed it again and closed! Pity the eyes that saw her swerve right and swerve left; that saw her trunk arch forward and straighten back up while the world watched breathless, not to miss a curve of the undulating body.

In the full grip of his fear and desire, he opened the door and she came in.

SHE: May I take off my coat?

HE *(thinking to himself)*: Even if she were a killer contracted to murder you, would there be a death more splendid than this? But you are not going to die. And the woman in front of you is not a killer, but a seeker of sex at any price. Kill you or not, what must never happen is for her to have you as a man. That would be more horrid than being slain by her. *(He contemplates her with eyes brimming with a thousand possibilities.)*

HE: So, you insist?
SHE: On what?
HE: Do you really not know?

SHE: I understand you. Actually I do insist still. But the objective has changed completely.

HE: Am I right then to assume that you are no longer interested in me as a client?

SHE: You can put it whichever way you like. Your problem, and mine with you, is that we do not speak the same language. In any case, my objective has changed.

HE: I don't believe your identity card and the story about you being a psychotherapist. Which organization . . . *(He was about to ask her which intelligence agency had forged the card for her so well. But he chose to act as if he had been fooled. Because if she had come from the CIA, FBI, Mossad, or the KGB, it would be stupid of him to expose her and let her know that he knew.)*

SHE: What organization? You suspect me, don't you? Your eyes say it, despite their stormy maritime green. I can read them to the very depth, as one sees a coin at the bottom of a perfectly still pond. What exactly are you thinking about me?

HE: Just read my mind! Don't you say you can see through my eyes to the depth? Why ask then?

SHE: Just to satisfy myself that my hunch is correct.

HE: And what is your hunch?

SHE: Well, that at the beginning of our encounter, you were just annoyed with me and reluctant to speak to me, but now I think you are beginning to be afraid of me.

He lets out a laugh, immediately realizing that it was louder than appropriate and completely hollow.

103

HE: Me? Afraid of a woman? A woman who is totally at my mercy? Ha! *(He is genuinely afraid.)*

SHE: May I sit down?

HE: Please, please!

(She sits, crossing her legs and causing her dress to retract, revealing her thighs.)

HE: You say your objective has changed and that you haven't come to seal the deal . . . and now you have shown me that identity of yours—why is it exactly that you are here?

She lies back in her armchair and only then does he notice that in addition to her handbag she carried a large tome elegantly bound. They are both silent for a while, as if the question on his mind was where to start; and on hers, why she was so interested in that man? Furtively, he reaches for the book. It looks like a PhD dissertation; typed and bound with a strange title, "Human Behavior in Animals." Author: Pamela Graham, followed by a sequence of title abbreviations, of which he only understood BA, Bachelor of Arts. Finally she speaks.

SHE: I've just found out your nationality.

(He is guiltily preoccupied with his attempt to look into her handbag, which drops open to the floor. They both collect the contents.)

HE: Found out what?

SHE: Your nationality.

HE: What is it then?
SHE: I'm not going to say . . .

There followed a long monologue by her of which he did not understand a word. His inner conflict was intensifying. He stared at her long legs. He was not used to such tall figures, which were uncommon in his country. Beautiful women there were mostly petite. But oh, those tapered thighs like an Arabian mare's! Like a sculpture. Not a blemish on her skin! Not a freckle! His pajama top that she borrowed was too inadequate for this magnificent figure, hiding only what could not be hidden. How splendid she looked as she sat, her covered arm resting on her bare legs.

New York: a city beyond legend. Its skyscrapers filled him with awe. They call it the modern jungle. What's terrifying about it is the smallness of man against the enormity of buildings. In New York one saw the excess of wealth and the excess of poverty, and nowhere else in the world were there as many prostitutes. Nor as many massage parlors and saunas. Women are freely advertised as if the city were a vast brothel. Therefore there was no avoiding that the protagonist of this novella should meet one of them, and that she should impose herself on him to the extent she did, despite all his beliefs and resistance. But was it just a question of prostitutes and prostitution? Or was she an agent for some organization? The thought didn't want to go away.

HE: May I ask you a rude question?

105

SHE: Isn't that what you've been doing from the beginning?

HE: Are you an agent for some organization?

She appeared to like the question, to savor it slowly as her facial expression suggested.

SHE: Suppose I am—do you think I'm already so head over heels in love with you that I will reveal myself? But let me tell you one thing: I have no problem working for any organization that pays generously. Money has become the number-one loyalty, and a life of luxury is what every downtrodden woman (and man) dreams of here in New York. Even if it means ending up in the electric chair. But—are you really that important?

HE *(to himself)*: True! I'm not important enough for them to assign my destruction to an agent disguised in the most abhorrent way to me: a prostitute. *(To her)* Every person is important in his own eyes.

SHE: I mean do you carry important secrets? I don't think so.

HE *(to himself)*: True again! I hold no secrets to justify a secret attempt on my life. All my 'secrets' are written and published.

SHE: Did you say something?

HE: Never mind! I often mutter to myself like a madman.

SHE: I do that too sometimes. Would you believe I've discovered that people are similar to an extent they cannot imagine?

HE *(like someone who has suddenly remembered something very serious)*: Is your name actually Pamela Graham?

SHE *(astonished)*: Yes, that's my name. What's strange about that?

HE: So, this book . . .

SHE: Oh, you mean this manuscript? It is my PhD dissertation. But I've made some changes in it and added new material, and I'm now trying to get it published.

HE: Is it also part of your 'work tools'?

SHE: What do you mean?

HE: In the old days, prostitutes used to exaggerate their makeup and wear revealing clothes to appear different from ordinary women. The fashion now, it seems, is for a prostitute to appear educated and to carry to bars or the 'workplace' the typescript of a book.

SHE: I'm not stupid enough to be offended by your words. Maybe you will never believe that it all happened by accident, but that's how it was. I left these (pointing at the dissertation and other papers) with my friend, the bartender, a few days ago, because I got a 'work' offer at a moment when I was least ready: I had been on my way to my room after seeing my literary agent. I didn't want to say no and I didn't want to take the stuff with me, so I left it with Joe. And it was he who reminded me of it tonight. *(She did not appear to be lying at all.)*

HE: Very well! Put on your clothes at once and let's go down to the bar.

Suddenly the man in him stood erect, like the genie out of the bottle. As if the manuscript was the female—that

107

dissertation, paragraph by paragraph and table by table. The scientist in her aroused the scientist in him, and that in turn aroused the man. His eyes were inflamed with his maleness. What happened next he could never quite understand. Was it the scientist in her that read with detachment the transformation in him before reacting to it sensually? Or was it her desire that grasped, rather late, the meaning of the fire in his eyes? There she stood toweringly tall, wearing his pajama top without the bottoms. When she got up to look for a match to light her cigarette, her shoulder touched his. For the first time, tall as he was, he felt a woman's shoulder as high as his. He, the upper half of his body naked without a pajama top; she, her lower half naked without the bottoms. He was losing control fast. But hers was a complete collapse. She fell to the ground on her knees and surrounded his waist with her arms, kissing any part of his body her lips could reach, and murmuring as if in a dream.

SHE: Well, you have completely crushed me and made me forget my work. *I* will pay you. How much would you accept?

The man in him overflowing with passion froze. As if with her sentence she had at the click of a button turned his depths into a block of ice. How much would he charge? The night began with how much she charged and was finishing with how much *he* charged. It was time to say goodbye forever to that amazingly tall figure and those breasts that protruded challengingly. In an anguished state, he lifted her with all his strength from her armpits and stood her on her feet. He spoke blows to her, wishing she were a man so he could deal her actual physical blows.

HE: Put on your clothes at once!
SHE: What's the matter? What happened? Why are you cross? I will pay you a lot. Whatever you ask for. And not just for tonight. For every night if you want. I'm yours. Say I've fallen in love with you . . . I've fallen in love with you. Please! I beg you.

She opened her handbag and took out her purse. But she froze with fear as she saw the intent to kill in his eyes. She turned pale like a wax statue. She started to put on her clothes in a frenzied hurry, as if one more moment of nakedness would herald her end.

They both were shaken by what had happened and too frightened to part. Again they must return to their sofa in the bar. To preserve his sanity he had to resume the conversation with her.

They are now back at the bar. Silence between them is total and charged. When they sit down, he is still shaken and distracted.

HE: You probably think that I don't believe you when you say that this is a dissertation for which you have

109

recently been awarded a PhD degree, and that you are a psychotherapist trained in psychology—well, actually I do believe you. But please, please, if you don't want me to go mad, give me a convincing answer to a simple question!

SHE: You mean the subject of my thesis, 'Human Behavior in Animals'?

HE *(exploding)*: Quite the contrary! I mean 'animal behavior in humans.' I mean the behavior of a human like you. An educated, knowledgeable woman. A perceptive intellectual who is not dying of hunger. How can such a woman of her own free will bring herself to work as a prostitute? Not just that, but when moved by desire, she does not hesitate to treat the man she desires as if he too were a prostitute for hire?

His sense of astonishment was always fresh. Always genuine. Always innocent. That a woman should willingly be a prostitute and take pride in it was jaw-droppingly unbelievable to him. Nor could he ever stomach that a man should be happy to touch, let alone have sex with, a woman he knows that all day hands, mouths, and bodies were taking turns over in a manner that inevitably deprived her of her individuality and therefore her femininity and her very humanity. For Dostoevsky whores were victims. They were Mary Magdalenes, crushed by circumstances and forced into selling their bodies. That he could accept and forgive. But actually for a woman to take pride in her trade to the point of unabashed open boastfulness; to actually prostitute her own feelings when they overcame her—that was something he could never ever imagine was possible, nor that a woman like that existed. And that was no simple woman led astray. Not a victim of Dostoevsky's wolfish men, but a woman with a doctorate, a researcher, a writer. The title of her thesis showed originality of thought. She was a woman who could be on a par with Freud and Madame Curie.

HE *(louder than before)*: How could you? How could you?

She makes herself comfortable in her seat, crossing her shapely, majestic legs. She fixes her gaze on him, appearing to have accepted the challenge.

SHE: What can I say to you? People grow up and yet continue to think like children. You disapprove of my job as prostitute, as if I was your mother caught sinning. My dear, sexual relations between man and woman have been a business deal since the beginning of history. It could be nothing else. Who pays doesn't matter. There were times when it was the woman who paid. In our time it is the other way around. Take the dowry or bride price that you call mahr, the engagement ring and the presents—in reality, what are these? Aren't these a price, a form of payment? I have studied marriage traditions in all religions and cultures. In each, I found there was a material deal struck for the marriage to happen.

HE: That may be so, but it's a deal for life. There's a big difference between this and . . .

SHE: And what?

HE: And the relationship becoming a mere business, a trade.

SHE: So, it's not an issue of principle? It's a question of the frequency of selling and buying? You accept my argument then?

HE: Not quite.

SHE: Okay, let us go by the norms of your romanticism, which obviously is bothering you. Let's assume it's a question of love. A passionate affair, as in the stories of Romeo and Juliet, or Richard Burton and Elizabeth Taylor. *You* invite your beloved for dinner and a dance at a nightclub, while Burton offers Taylor a diamond ring worth a million dollars. Yes?

HE: I would say it's a shared invitation; we invite each other and share the cost, the English way.

SHE: You mean you share and no one is buying the other? Fine, but in the end you want to make her happy and you are thinking of buying her a present, right? What does that mean? It means you want to say to her "In return for the pleasure you have given me, dear, take this!' Or she to you, "Here, darling, in return for your love."

HE: Yes, but it's a gift.

SHE: A price. The scientific name is 'price.' For every pleasure there is a price. The principle therefore is valid.

HE: But these are private relations, accompanied with very intimate feelings. There's a big difference between me writing a love poem for my beloved and making photocopies of it to distribute to scores of women.

SHE: Not really. There's no difference. It's only a question of duration.

HE: Duration?

SHE: A love story used to span an entire novel. And a novel used to span a whole lifetime. Love stories have grown shorter. As short as six months in the novels of Françoise Sagan. For me, the longest takes one night.

HE: But you do not love, you trade.

SHE: Not true. Your information about prostitutes is very out of date. We live the age of the ultra-modern prostitute. You saw for yourself how I turned down three jobs, and I could have declined more. And if it weren't for your old-fashioned ideas, you would have experienced pleasure as you have never known in your life. I choose who I like.

HE: Choose?

SHE: Of course, because my first goal is my own enjoyment.

HE: A human being, ma'am or doctor, is first and foremost a bundle of values. Is this no longer the case in New York? No more values here? Only the dollar and selfish personal pleasure?

SHE: The dollar is a value—that's true. As for pleasure, what's wrong with having pleasure, if I'm also giving pleasure to another party and harming no one?

HE: Have you not thought, with all your learning, about humankind? If all women did what you do, won't this be the beginning of the end of the human race?

113

SHE: Not at all. It may actually be the beginning of the end for a lot of hypocrisy that stands in the way of human progress. If my psychological makeup is as I have explained to you, and then I'm forced to marry, have children, and be faithful to my husband, the result would be that I would commit adulteries greater in number than the hair on my husband's head, and give birth to children that I don't want and who won't love me. And so another miserable family producing more miserable generations will be added to your so-called 'humankind.' This matter should be entirely optional. Some women like to be wives and mothers, and, like you, cannot imagine multiple relationships—very well, those are indeed the good wives who can enrich humankind with children who are wanted and loved. Why is it obligatory that all women should marry all men, and that all married women and men should have children? Who has decreed this one model for human existence? Why can't there be another model in which everyone can have their preference? If men like women, fine. If women like men, fine. If men like men, fine. If women like women, fine. If a woman does not want marriage, let her have her wish. If another craves a permanent bond and children, let her also have her wish. Why this weird inhuman obsession to apply one way of life to four billion people, of whom not two, just two, are similar.

These loud calls for individual freedom for men and women have been known to him since the 1960s. He has been involved in debates and arguments about it in Europe and America, and even in Russia and some countries of the Arabian Peninsula. But allowing maximum individual freedom is one thing and charging a price for it is another.

HE: *(He conveyed for her the above stream of thought.)*
SHE: You are such a moralist.
HE: Morality means being true to yourself, and that, in my opinion, is the highest point of civilization.
SHE: By that reckoning, I'm very much a moralist too.
HE: How—when you are . . . ?
SHE: Let me tell you something. You know, my dear, that I'm a psychotherapist, as my job is known now. I assume you know what psychotherapists do?
HE: I suppose they carry out daily treatment as prescribed by the psychiatrist.
SHE: Something like that. And my specialization was and still is the treatment of male impotence.
HE: Impotence!
SHE: Yes. In recent years there has been an increase in such cases, and many clinics now specialize in their treatment. It seems that the emancipation of the western woman (and maybe women everywhere), and her assertion of her will over the man's will, has had an effect on men's sexual potency, which has been declining. My work as a psychotherapist is to help those men regain their potency.

His curiosity was aroused. That was the first time he had heard of clinics dedicated to that kind of psychological therapy and that female doctors and therapists undertook this work.

HE: And how do you help them?

SHE: First I have to make sure you understand some facts. There is no such thing as impotence, unless there is a physiological reason for erectile dysfunction. Otherwise, it is all psychological, because scientifically a man can have sex as long as he is alive. Of course energy and frequency decrease but never cease altogether. In my clinic we practiced both psychological and physical treatment that brought potency back to many of our patients. My specialization was to undertake physical therapy. You cannot imagine how happy I was every time a patient of mine regained his potency. Their gratitude went as far as inviting me to their golden and diamond jubilees and showering me with gifts and affection.

HE: How wonderful! Truly a noble and very useful scientific achievement.

SHE: And do you find much difference between my current job, which you call prostitution, and what I used to do in the clinic?

HE: Of course! What you did at the clinic was scientific therapy.

SHE: And what is it that I do now? Isn't what I do often, indeed most of the time, therapy? But you are right: there is a difference between the two jobs; a difference that made me opt for my current one.

HE: And what's that?

SHE: At the clinic I was paid exactly five dollars per hour. Now, I earn a hundred and maybe more per hour.

She ended that statement with a laugh, while he looked dumbfounded for a moment, like one over-whelmed by a sudden discovery. Then he burst out laughing. He guffawed boisterously, doubled over and smacked his thighs, until he began to attract attention despite the place being crowded and noisy. Finally he stopped and began to speak very calmly.

HE: Indeed! What's the difference? Or, rather the differ-ence is big. Very big. *(He falls silent, and remains silent for a long time. The silence between them spreads until it engulfs the thronged place and the giant city outside. As if everything had dropped dead. Then very slowly he begins to speak again.)* Indeed there is a difference. To practice therapy for treatment is one thing, and for money is another. The first they call work, the second prostitution.

SHE: The same thing, different names. Bullshit!

HE *(resuming his speech, which was no longer mere conversation but a statement of his credo in life)*: Woman, the female of humankind, who took millions of years of changes and adjustments until she became the zenith of evolutionary life, the most beautiful of God's cre-ation—*you* want to reverse the evolution of that human female, cancel out millions of years of evolvement? You want to hurl her back into the

117

abyss where evolution had stopped with cats, dogs, and mice? Even with those animals, sex is obtained heroically: two male cats fight over a female and the winner gets her. She becomes the prize, the medal, deserved by the victor, and asks for no return; she does not turn into a commodity. She just gives, and gives liberally what you measure in hours and dollars; what you turn into a profession for earning the most money in the least time. But you've got it wrong, because if we were to stretch the metaphor, you are misusing yourself as capital. In order to make a quick buck, you lose so much of your capital, of yourself, of your soul. You lose everything. You lose your very belonging to the kind.

SHE: What a great sermon! And what do you mean by 'losing my kind'? Do I become a man for instance?

HE: No. You lose your belonging to humankind altogether.

SHE: You mean I become an animal?

HE: But animals do not do what you do. Nothing, nobody in nature is created to be on offer for sale. We come into life in order to evolve constantly toward what is higher and nobler.

SHE: "What's higher and nobler"—I know these words well. They are just words. Your words, my uncles', my neighbors'. Always said behind the back, as if they were ashamed of them. What's higher and nobler indeed! Why should evolution happen according to Your Excellency's point of view? Why can't it be happening according to mine?

HE: And what's yours, Lady Darwin?

SHE: For me, "the higher and nobler" is the one who earns the most money with the least effort.

HE: Do you really think that the great call for freedom and liberalization can become a justification for treating the human body in an inhuman way? Is this what you call freedom?

SHE: Yes: my freedom to sell myself.

HE: This is not freedom. It turns a human being into a commodity, into a dealer in white slavery. It turns you into a trader who deals not in the bodies of others but your own. You offer yourself like any goods with a price label. He who can afford can buy. Can you imagine that? The buyer obtains you. The whole of you. He obtains your soul with its most intimate parts. He penetrates into your secret of secrets.

SHE: A client may imagine that, but I only allow them what I want to allow them.

HE: Can you then stop a deal in the middle and cancel it?

SHE: I haven't had to so far. But I'm sure the moment I need to, I will do it.

HE: No, ma'am. You will never do it. This is not a step that's possible for a woman who's turned into merchandise. For a woman to do that, she needs to be free and proud. She needs to be a woman of integrity and a will of her own, and not one who sells herself to every Tom, Dick, and Harry.

SHE: But we all are merchandise in the jobs that we do. And mine is just a job like any other.

119

HE: Absolutely not! Yours is not just a job from which to earn a living. It is a crime against yourself by which you lay waste to your humanity. What you do is not a job and nothing can justify it: feelings cannot be for sale. Have you ever heard of a human being crying for a fee? Being joyous for payment? Or charging by the hour for being angry? We are people, not playthings. We are talking about the human being that your so-called 'first world' regrettably turned into a commodity, a cog in an enormous production and consumption machine called society. And since all jobs are alike in dehumanizing us, thus moving from one job to another becomes a matter of no concern. But it's not as simple as that: you did not just switch from a job called 'therapist' to another called 'prostitute': you switched from a noble job that builds up your soul as the healer of patients to one that brings ruin to your soul, that eats you alive. You have lodged your soul in a body that is up for rental like furnished apartments with ten percent added for service. *And* it is a body that offers excellent accommodation because the owner is an educated, sophisticated therapist guaranteed to attract lodgers to her apartments. To put it mildly, I will say you are a patient who pretends to be a therapist; you are more ill than your clients. You seek to fill the emptiness inside you by looking for affection in the embraces of clients who only serve to make you feel your emptiness all the more.

SHE: A patient? You call love a disease?

HE: Do you call what you do 'love'?

SHE: Why then do you think I've chosen it?

HE: Because you are actually sick. A healthy person will allow no one to touch them—just touch them—unless they give permission. As for you, when you declare yourself a prostitute, even a part-time prostitute, it is as if you've put up a sign saying, "Please touch! Please feel! Free trial!" A woman who does that must be sick in the mind.

SHE *(sarcastically)*: So, I'm sick, Doctor? I wonder which of us really is the sick one? Why can't you be the sick one, with all those ideas that throng your head, all those principles and morals? Yes, why can't it be the other way around?

HE: I, Madam *(stressing it this time)*, am very civilized because I believe that mankind is not only the most sublime being but also the most dangerous, even to himself. That being needs to be always pure, no specks of dirt should be allowed to stick to that thing encased in his skull, or else he would turn into the basest being in existence. Because he will be using his brain, the most sublime product of creative evolution, against creative evolution itself; he will be using it for destruction. He will destroy himself and those around him, even his most beloved ones.

SHE: But I'm happy, and I make everyone happy that chance brings my way.

HE: You lie to yourself. You can't be happy at the disgust you see in every face you meet.

SHE: I make love, therefore I am.

HE: Unfortunately you *are*, but not because you make love. In fact, you just *are*. You merely exist. You do not know the sweetest and most splendid kind of existence: to love and be loved. "I make love, therefore I am" indeed! Would a little girl love her doll or kitten in return for money? Do you not feel you exist except when selling love, when defiling your body and bashing your pride? Are you blind to your behavior? Is all you can see in the world a man's wallet and the tariff per hour? This is the inevitable end of the road when the only criterion of value for a man or woman is the dollar-per-hour one. Prostitution is the inescapable outcome.

A woman like you will never see the face of a man tenderly embracing her and looking at the reflection of their image together in the mirror. A man chosen by her, his features chosen by her, and ending up liking in him that of which at first she did not approve. A man who also singled her out of many because he prized her qualities above all others. A man who satisfies her and is satisfied by her. A man who respects her and is respected by her. A man with all his roots, his space, his sky, standing under the light of the universe. You will never see the face of your child as he or she steals his way into your image in the mirror encircling your legs with his arms; his features from you both; his sharp temper from you and his naughtiness from his father. A child born out of a moment of harmony between the two of you, and nature, and the whole universe; a moment that kindled the spark that now was a living form between the two of you. There are many things that you don't see. You can't even see yourself.

SHE: You talk to me as if you were addressing humanity from the top of the Eiffel Tower. Honor, truth, the sublime human being—where do you find these things on this earth that's sunk in mire? What can I do when I was born into a jungle not of my making? What can I do but preserve my existence, secure a place to live, food, and some pleasure for myself, and if I can't, then steal or kill for them? You may have the luxury to live honorably but others do not have that luxury.

HE: You lie to yourself. You are wearing a ring that in my country would be enough to sustain a whole family for three years. You are not really that starved.

SHE: Hunger in your country is the simplest kind of hunger: an animal need for food. But my hunger is a human being's hunger for life: the hunger to live a life of enjoyment. Life for mere existence is the lowly life of animals. I'm hungry for travel and a life full of pleasure. My hunger and that of people like me here is not the hunger of the stomach. It is the hunger of the lofty centers of the brain, of imagination and dreams, of high impulses, my dear sir.

HE: And for these "high impulses" you descend so low with your body, lower than animals?

SHE: So be it! I descend to the animal in me in order to indulge all that makes me a human being.

123

HE: And by so doing you lose both the animal and the human being, because a human being cannot rise above his animality. A human being becomes human only when the animal in him is satisfied. The animal in him must respect his animality in order for the human in him to be able to celebrate his humanity. A skyscraper cannot rise on a foundation of mire, no matter how much its upper stories are crammed with ornaments, lights, and decorations.

SHE: You mean it needs a foundation of the kind you call 'high values'?

HE: And which you call 'animal qualities.' What life of pleasure is that in which, like Shylock's debt, you pay back out of your flesh and blood? You become like a heroin addict who sells one of his fingers every day in return for his fix. Permit me to say, ma'am, that you are very sick, and your sickness has led you to believe in a kind of life that you know in your depths is a lie, a falsity, self-deceit.

SHE: You are beginning to bore me.

HE: That's because I've gotten too close to your vulnerable core. You've created for yourself, as you say, the perfect life. You love men and you love to change men, and into the bargain you make money and spend a good time. Everyday a new face and a new body. But one day you will wake up to find nothing new at all. Not even someone to say "Good morning" to you. I'd say you are about thirty now—I wonder how many people will come to your forty-fifth or even fortieth birthday party?

SHE: You are really becoming very boring. What do you want from me? What do you hold against me?

HE: The very thing you boast about: that you are a prostitute.

SHE: But you too are a prostitute. And all those clean-shaven, smiling men, who speak with polite, hushed voices—all those men and women around you are prostitutes.

HE: Me? A prostitute?

SHE: Of course, you are. What is it again you do for a living? I forget—ah! A writer, you said. You probably work for some institution in a society that supports you and pays you a salary—do you say the truth, all that you believe to be the truth to that society? Or do you say some things and hide others? Is this not prostitution? The lawyer who defends a man in the full knowledge that he is a thief or murderer to get his fee—what do you call him? The politician who sells his country or turns a blind eye to its interests—what do you call him? The judge who takes bribes; the wife who cannot bear to look at her husband but moans lovingly when he touches her; the son who hates his father but shows his respect to him every morning— what do you call all of them? What do you call the scientists who invent weapons of mass destruction? The politicians who take their countries to war? The writers who know the truth but are afraid to speak it? Isn't all this prostitution? All of you are prostitutes, highly paid prostitutes, but I'm the only one nailed to the cross. I'm the only sinner among you, and you just the stone-throwers.

HE: Again this is lying to yourself. All you say is correct, but selling one's body is something else.

SHE: What I do is the least harmful. Since we are all prostitutes, the best among us are those who cause the least damage. At least I only harm myself, if you call what I do harm. As for the prostitute who cheats millions, ravishes the beliefs of millions, robs millions, and kills millions. . . . *(She falls silent for a moment, then starts to talk again slowly and in a low voice that gradually rises.)* I have wasted the night in a futile conversation. My life will not be changed by a chance encounter with some man. I have already chosen my life. What a waste of a night!

HE: Maybe a night has been wasted but a life saved?

SHE: Preaching again?

HE: No. But I'm sure you will be thinking about what I've said.

SHE: I don't care one bit for what you have said. I've chosen my life. I'm a prostitute but I'm clean. I don't claim to be Mrs. So-and-so, the girlfriend of so-and-so, or the widow of so-and-so. I am clean: I say to everyone "I'm a prostitute." With this public declaration, I become cleaner than you all. I do not lie to you or to myself. *You* are the liars, and lying is dishonorable; it is the true prostitution. I am a prostitute but I am clean.

HE: No, ma'am. Don't con yourself, if you want to live up to your claim of honesty. Admit that selling one's body is the most despicable act a human being could commit.

Admit too that you don't know why you do it and don't take shelter behind generalizations. Admit to yourself that you are going to self-destruct and that you need treatment; you need someone to stand by your side.

SHE *(warningly)*: I am clean. Clean.

Her raised voice attracts attention. The headwaiter approaches with his tall figure and his austere, melancholic features. He slows down when he reaches their table and suddenly smiles idiotically from the context of his austere face.

THE HEADWAITER: You appear a little nervous tonight, Doctor . . .

SHE *(in a voice still extremely loud)*: I am clean.

THE HEADWAITER: I know very well that pay is miserable in those clinics and university hospitals—why don't you work full-time here, or wherever you like? It must be such a strain to have two jobs. Don't you agree, sir?

HE *(looking at her)*: Is that what you do?

SHE: Yes, yes. I will focus on one job. I will focus on cleanliness. Because I am clean. More clean than all of you.

The headwaiter is dumbfounded. Petrified. She is now screaming. She jumps to her feet suddenly and nervously collects her handbag, book, and papers.

SHE *(screaming full blast)*: I'm clean. Clean. No, I'm dirty. Very dirty. But I say it. I scream it. I'm very clean because I'm very, very dirty. I'm the cleanest of the dirty. I'm cleaner than all of you. Bullshit!

The bar is submerged in utter silence, the clientele appearing shell-shocked. Only the sound of her hurried footsteps as she stormed out of the place could be heard. Gradually soft whispers begin to be heard, and continue to rise and rise. The stunned faces begin to restore their smiles and laughter begins to ring: the bar is back to its normal level of noise, as if nothing had happened.

He cups his chin between the palms of his hands and fixes his gaze on the remotest corner of the universe.

HE: When, Lord, will you give some men the courage of some prostitutes?

THE SECRET OF HIS POWER

1

My relationship with the sultan was limited to an incurious glance in his direction as I came and went, just a quick glance as if to reassure myself he was there. For he was a major landmark of the village, like the railway station, the Nasif family mansion, and the haunted spot where Sayyid Ibrahim was murdered.

One day, however, I was obliged to concern myself with the sultan. It was the day I achieved the first success of my life by passing the first-year exams at the elementary school. My joy at succeeding on that day was to remain greater than any sense of achievement later in life. On that day I wished I could return home carried on the wings of a bird to convey the news to my great-grandfather, the grandfather of my father. He was very old with a badly curved back and innumerable gentle wrinkles that covered his face, neck, chest, and whole body. In their abundance and uniformity they looked as if he had been born with them.

"You must honor your pledge immediately," said my great-grandfather in his serious voice as soon as he heard the news.

I had forgotten the story of the pledge completely. It so happened that during the year I fell into a sense of deep despair while studying and became certain that whatever I did, I was not going to succeed. I was on the verge of tears when I went to my great-grandfather and made him an extra-sweet cup of coffee (the way he liked it) and carried it to him secretly. He loved coffee but his son, my immediate grandfather, forbade him to drink it. Thus we made an agreement: I would smuggle some ground coffee and sugar for him and we would find a remote corner to make a cup for him. In return he would talk to me, after clearing his head with the coffee, about the good old days. On that day I brought him the coffee and waited until he had drunk it all sip by sip and licked all the dregs of the cup, then I asked him if he thought I was going to pass my exams. The strange thing was that I was sure that my great-grandfather had no idea about schools, exams, and success, yet when he said to me that God willing I was going to succeed, I was overjoyed and became certain that I was going to pass. However, he insisted that day that I pledge to light, upon success, half a dozen candles at the shrine of Sultan Hamid, and he would not let me go until I solemnly reiterated the pledge in front of him several times.

It was no problem to obtain the money for the candles: I had passed my exams and no request of mine on that day was likely to meet with objection. But I will never forgive myself for giving in to the devil's temptation when I went to the shop. In truth it was not the devil, but the jar of hard candies standing on the service counter. I split the money in half. With one I bought only three candles, and with the other, candy. And as I was making my way to the edge of the cemetery where the shrine stands, I was still blaming myself and I imagined that Sultan Hamid would take his revenge on me for the three usurped candles by haunting me in my sleep or afflicting me with jaundice.

I don't know if this was the reason for my nervousness, or something else, for I had begun to feel very disturbed when the cemetery appeared in the distance and I was able to make out the shrine of Sultan Hamid. It was a strange thing, this, because I had seen Sultan Hamid's shrine in the distance before without caring about it. I couldn't even tell its color. Nor did I care in any measure about the sultan. Yet so nervous was I, that I thought many times of turning around and sprinting back home. Especially because that 'pledge' thing had not really entered into my head, I was sure that that sultan had nothing to do with my success. He had not helped me with English, nor did he smuggle me the answer to the long-division question. Indeed, pledges to saints, the jinn, or inhaling the scent of onion on Shamm al-Nasim in the spring and the like were things I did not believe in. Not because we were taught at school that they were false beliefs inspired by Satan, but because everyone took them for granted. How could *I* do that? And what would be the use of my education and the suit I wore?

Despite my increasing nervousness, I did not turn back. Not for fear of my grandfather, but for fear of finding myself a coward: it seems as children we are no less shy of running away than as adults. Thus I forged on, fearful but defiant of my fear, driven by the excitement of a new experience, until I arrived at the shrine of Sultan Hamid. It stood in a corner of the cemetery, adjacent to a desolate road. It was the first time for me to see the shrine at close quarters. It wasn't really a shrine in the true sense of the word. The people of our village called it maqam, a term less grand than shrine. They were right because it did not remotely resemble the splendid saints' shrines in Cairo that I had visited with my father, with their thick plush carpets, gilded grillwork, enormous chandeliers, and that mysterious scent that filled their atmosphere and inspired awe and piety. As for the sultan's maqam, it was no more than an old room, as if built at the beginning of time, and from whose walls the paint had peeled, disclosing their red worn stones, like the ribs of a decayed corpse. Nothing distinguished the maqam from other tombs except being built of stone while most were built of mud brick. Only the rich had their tombs plastered and had the names of their dead inscribed on them by Mr. Muhammad al-Banna, who wrote the names in blue paint with his awkward inept hand.

There was another distinguishing factor between the maqam and the other tombs. Unlike the others, around the maqam stood tall camphor trees. They too seemed to have been there since time began. They are endlessly tall with thick trunks that not even a giant could encircle in a hug. In their regular spacing they formed high imposing walls around the maqam.

Everything called on me to finish my task and go home quickly. Evening was descending and shadows elongated frightfully. Beyond, the vast wheat fields looked like a white shoreless sea in which people appeared like tiny dark spots, almost invisible.

I went around the maqam, which had only an old faded door and a single window. That must be the window about which my grandfather had told me. I approached it but before reaching it, I was taken aback by the pools and rivulets of solidified wax covering the ground: the melted wax of the pledged candles, burnt over the years for the sultan, had covered the window sill and streamed down the wall covering its bare stones until it reached the ground.

I realized that thousands before me must have pledged candles for Sultan Hamid, or perhaps millions. Though, in a child's mind, millions does not always mean millions.

I nearly laughed at the innocence of the people of my village, whose money had melted and congealed into the dust. What for? For this sultan who had no mosque, no servant, and no followers. Not even a shrine that inspired respect.

I was on the point of turning back and keeping the candles for my friends and me to play with. How exciting, how beautiful, I thought, it would be to light them at night and sit in their glare! I even blamed myself for wasting money on the candles instead of buying more sweets, and for allowing myself to behave the way the ignorant people of my village did—those illiterates.

Nevertheless, that day I only kept one candle and lit up the other two. I don't know why. Maybe just in obedience to my great-grandfather's instructions. Or maybe out of a desire to imitate the people of my village. Just imitation. Indeed, why don't I admit that after reciting the Fatiha of the Qur'an, and praying for my father and grandfather, I pledged to light up a full dozen of candles for the sultan if I succeeded the following year. And although I told myself on my way home that I had only pledged the dozen candles because I thought it was a lucky thing to do, the fact is that from that day on, Sultan Hamid began to preoccupy my thoughts.

Sometimes I pitied him—that poor holy man buried in that desolate spot. I also thought of those who believed in him, who were poor like him, who made their little innocent wishes and lifted their eyes to the sky, pledging candles for him, and when the sultan made their wishes come true, they would hasten to his window to light their candles. And night after night, the sultan's window would shimmer with the light of a candle: a little wish that had come true; a poor heart that experienced a moment of happiness, if only for one night. Sometimes I thought too of the huge amount of wax hardened by the maqam. How come nobody thought of stealing it? Especially as the sultan had no servant in attendance and the way to him was empty of passersby, and people in our village would normally not leave the merest pebble or rock lying on the ground without picking it up if they thought it could be of use at home.

In those days I would sometimes think of recruiting a gang of my friends to plunder the wax, but then fear would hold me back. The sultan's name did not crop up in conversation much, and when it did, it was not necessarily accorded excessive veneration. No one, for instance, would interrupt conversation to indulge in a pious recitation of the Fatiha on mention of his name. A man would clap together his sandals to shed excessive dust as he got up, saying, "This is neither here nor there. Help us, O Sultan Hamid, help us!" Or a woman would squat in front of the fish basket, saying to Mr. Ali, the fisherman, "How much?", and he would say, "Ten piasters." Then she would say, "And for the sake of Sultan Hamid, for how much?", at which Mr. Ali would look down, closing his eyes as if utterly defeated, and say, "For the sultan, eight piasters, but for you, nine." Or again, if a man was lifting a heavy sack of flour to put away over his wife's head, saying, "Give me strength, O Sultan Hamid!"

I understood the people of my village well enough. The permanent scowl on their faces did not concern me, nor their thorny beards and the ruthless look in their eyes, for I understood them inside out, and knew that they did not say what they thought except between themselves. In front of the village chief or government officials, they would let off a lot of hot air, loudly, and swear by God most vehemently, and if a stranger asked them about something, their answer would be the opposite of what they really thought. Only unwittingly would they reveal what lay in their depths. In scattered words. In whispers behind the backs of government officials. Or in a man's chat with his wife after supper, when he would rest his back against the wall and stretch his legs in front of him, saying, "I had a good dream last night, woman. Make it good, O Lord! Sultan Hamid came to me in my sleep and said to me, 'Why are you still sleeping until noon? Get up! The sun has risen. Get up!'"

2

used to take pity on the people of our village. I had
visited the sultan and seen his maqam at close quarters
but I had felt no awe. I did not tremble. My hair did
not stand on end. Nor did I witness any miracles by him.
Only four old walls, close to collapsing. What was there
between those walls to make their inhabitant dwell at the
center of the people's hearts, and to make them speak
about him as if he were a gigantic being living somewhere? What was there about him to make them talk
about him so familiarly, as if he were a close neighbor? I
knew the full significance of this familiarity, because peasants rarely dropped formality, and when they addressed
you without titles or spoke to you as they would to a
neighbor, it meant that their respect for you was verging
on sanctification.

In truth I had started to be jealous of Sultan Hamid.
I began to envy him the place he had in people's hearts
when in reality he could do nothing for them. That struc-
ture of stone standing at the edge of the cemetery—how
could it attract all this veneration?

One day I told myself that I might be wrong; that there might be something inside the maqam to justify that status. I had not, in my general disregard for the sultan, cared to cast a glance on the inside through the window when I lit the candles. I rebuked myself greatly for not having done that, and decided to put things right. But I did not hasten to act on the idea, because the matter of Sultan Hamid didn't bother me to that extent. Those were just thoughts that occurred to me when he cropped up in conversation: I would then think about him a little before forgetting him again.

But one Friday morning I heard a woman in the street bemoaning her fortune. She was on the verge of tears each time she told the story of her ill son to whoever stopped for her, and each time she ended the story on a pledge of a dozen candles for the sultan if her son recovered from his illness. I nearly stepped out into the street to tell her off and explain to her that that Sultan Hamid of hers had nothing to do with the illness of her son, that he could do nothing for him, that he could not even ward off decay from his own maqam. But I held back and asked myself candidly why something like that irritated me. What harm was there in the woman pledging some candles for the sultan? Would the pledge prevent her son's recovery if he was fated to recover? I realized that my annoyance was at her mention of the name of Sultan Hamid in particular, and not, for instance, mine. My annoyance was at my increasing realization of the status the sultan enjoyed in the hearts of the people of our village. I feared for myself. I feared that the day might come when I too would believe in him, and hold him in reverence without knowing why.

Thus, by way of emphasizing my disapprobation of the sultan, I decided to make my way to the maqam on the spot to look at it from inside, and unravel the so-called mystery. Then I would be able to laugh uninhibitedly at both the sultan and the people of our village.

But something happened. For when I drew closer to the maqam and saw the rivulets and pools of frozen wax, I felt I was about to commit a sin. I felt like I was going to tamper with something that belongs to the entire community of our village in their absence; as if I were in a massive public meeting and was about to tear up the national flag of those present. Thus I stood in my place, in a state of hesitancy, feeling for the first time that I was about to do something forbidden. I kept looking around me, though I was certain the place was empty and that nobody came there in the morning.

I was afraid.

For only then did I realize that Sultan Hamid was an enormous giant, thanks to the people of our village who had made him into one. Although I was frozen in my place, powerless to approach the window, I was nonetheless unable to fathom the situation and the fact that I actually did not dare come closer. Maybe it was fear that impelled me to look again at Sultan Hamid's maqam. Everything was exactly the same as in the previous visit: the old dilapidated room, and the stone walls with the flaking paintwork. Nothing at all to instill fear. Everything I saw inspired contempt. Thus I approached the window stealthily. It was higher than I was tall, and in order to see what was inside I had to grab the iron bars of the grill and lift myself.

I clung to the iron bars. They were cold and slippery from the wax congealed on them. I lifted myself in one leap then immediately let myself down, my heart pounding. I had seen nothing but all-encompassing darkness, yet I was frightened. Dark at daytime and inside Sultan Hamid's maqam was a terrifying thing.

I still clung on to the iron bars, waiting to regain my breath to cast another glance. I had absolutely no idea as to what I might see inside. Maybe the maqam was empty. Maybe there was only darkness.

Forcefully I lifted myself high and, scared stiff, turned my eyes quickly around the place. Terror made my hair stand on end. I was too terrified even to descend. My hands just froze on the window bars and I closed my eyes so as not to see and started to scream in panic. Breathless and on the point of dying, I let myself fall to the ground.

I saw Sultan Hamid himself inside. He was huge, bigger than a camel, and had a very long neck, which frightfully stemmed from his immense body, ending in a large green mass that shimmered in the dark. The Sultan was sitting inside like a camel chewing on something, and he nearly stretched his long neck and snapped my head off.

I sat there my head hidden in my lap and my eyes closed. I was not able to run or think or even say the name of God, the Merciful, the Compassionate. Around me were thousands of the afreets, in whom I had never believed, Satan, my jinn sisters who lived underground, and all the sins I had committed and the beliefs I had mocked.

I thought that I was going to die presently, and was amazed when a long time had passed without that happening. Then I laughed at myself for thinking that I was going to die. Then I opened my eyes and I saw the tall camphor trees and the fields in the expanse beyond and the people going and coming there like daytime stars. Everything was unafraid and everything scoffed at me and my fear.

Then I found myself thinking about the one thing I thought could never happen: why not take another look at the maqam?

I looked up at the window hesitantly. But soon I found myself propelled by an irresistible urge to cling to those iron bars again. Maybe it was fear. Maybe curiosity. Or just contempt for the sultan. We were a devilish generation, as our parents and grandparents said. Mysterious issues of afreets and the like were things that we only talked about. We did not believe in them in our heart of hearts, though we might remember them at the moment of drowning. Our parents used to say that about us because we were not afraid of the things they were afraid of. And even when we were afraid, our fear only caused us to laugh at the very thing we feared. We were a generation of devils who played soccer instead of handball, and who walked on the forbidden railroad tracks without fear of a train suddenly appearing and running them over, and even when a train appeared they would just step aside and pelt it with pebbles, before going back on the railroad track.

3

was right. The camel-like thing sitting inside was not
Sultan Hamid, but his tomb; its long neck, the tombstone; and the shimmering green thing, the sultan's
turban on top of the stone. Moreover, the cloth cover over
the tomb was so old and faded you could hardly make it
out from the layers of dust settled on it. The verses from the
Qur'an woven into the fabric had been eaten by moths, and
a rotten smell wafted from the room. The prevailing darkness did not look like darkness, but rather an ancient light;
light that had been buried for so long, it became darkness.

I went back with a big chunk of wax that I cut out of
the ground and dusted off, hoping it would be good for
something. But when at home, I was at a loss as to what
to do with it. First I made a ball, then a water jug, but
finally I found myself unconsciously shaping it into a
tomb with a long tombstone and a green turban.

I liked my statue of the tomb so much that I would
neither discard it nor try to reshape the wax. All I wanted
was to keep it somewhere safe. After long consideration,
I settled on one of the holes in our pigeon tower.

Nonetheless, I stopped thinking about Sultan Hamid, and was amazed at myself for it. My intellect just refused to tackle his problem. I felt him totally alien to me, as if he had never crossed my mind. As if I had never heard of him or concerned myself with his story. Sometimes I would try to force myself to think about him, but to no avail. I would say to myself that maybe tomorrow I would think about him. But tomorrow would come and I would not be thinking about him. A very long period passed—maybe a year, maybe several years—without Sultan Hamid crossing my mind. Could the human mind take that long to turn its attention to a subject?

Be that as it may, one morning I woke up to find myself thinking about Sultan Hamid. It was a different line of thought that time. Was he from our village? If so, of which family was he? And who were his descendants?

I went around asking those questions of the oldest survivors of our village. They were unanimous that Sultan Hamid was not related to anyone in our village. They thought he might have been a stranger, but no one could tell with any accuracy. All they knew was that our village had produced no holy men, and that no maqam had ever been built for one of its dead.

They had no idea how astonished their answers left me. If Sultan Hamid was a stranger, why did he choose our village to be buried in? And who built for him that maqam of stone when all the tombs of the village were built of mud brick? Who bought the fabric cover? Who made that long tombstone and fixed the turban on top of it? Who planted those tall camphor trees?

The strangest thing of all was the way in which the elders of my village received my questions. They would listen to me as if I were out of my mind to pose such questions. It was as if I were asking who dug the sea, or gave our village its name. Why should I ask them about a thing that was there before they were born—a thing that they grew up to find in existence, and that was likely to remain in existence until Judgment Day?

I in turn marveled at their attitude and had no doubt they were the crazy ones. How could it be that it never occurred to them to find out why Sultan Hamid was buried in our village rather than any other, and why a maqam was built for him?

We would argue for long stretches. Me, in my city-style outfit, my uncovered head, and my uninhibited readiness to delve into any subject; they, with their long beards, diminished eyesight, and adherence to convention. Even my great-grandfather—no matter how many cups of coffee I made him; no matter how long I waited for his head to clear and for the smile to come back to his face—as soon as I opened my mouth to ask a question, he would say, "I told you a hundred times to think only about things that can benefit you. Think about your studies! What business of yours are these things?"

When I felt I was close to making my great-grandfather angry, I would pretend to agree with him. But I had never been persuaded, because the questions I was asking about Sultan Hamid were ones that no man in his right senses could ignore. A giant like him who had a following in every household and whose name is constantly invoked by all and sundry, and whose status no one, living or dead, could aspire to—and yet no one knew anything about him, and no one wanted to know anything about him? Wasn't this enough to drive one crazy? Or at least angry? And what could be more cause for anger than the complete indifference with which the young and old of the village met me when I presented them the questions that perplexed me?

I began to be fed up with Sultan Hamid and even more so with the people of our village. It was as if he had amassed a fortune to which he had no right. As if they had surrendered their meager possessions to make him rich. Just like that. Stupidly.

On one occasion I put the question to Shaykh Shaltut, who ran the kuttab of the village, but I was wasting my time. I knew that asking him would lead to nowhere. Every time I asked him about anything, I was rewarded with nothing but a worthless answer. I asked him why Sultan Hamid was held in such high status by the people.

"Because he was a pious man," he said.

"So you must know about him—tell me!" I said.

"All I know is that he must have been a good man, else he wouldn't have a maqam," he said.

"But his maqam is modest and dilapidated. Nothing like the shrines of al-Sayyida Zaynab or al-Husayn," I said.

"It's not a question of the grandeur of the shrine, son. Rather, it's his status with God," he said.

"What should I do then to discover the secret of Sultan Hamid?" I said.

"By getting closer to God. By mention of God's name," came the answer.

I thought much about what he said, despite its uselessness. In fact, I found myself often visiting him at his kuttab and indulging in discussions with him which at no time brought me any closer to solving the sultan's mystery.

I convinced myself that maybe what he said was correct. Maybe the secret of Sultan Hamid could only be revealed to special people, to the good. Maybe if I were to mention the name of God and draw closer to Him— maybe then I would arrive at a place from which I could see the sultan and understand his secret. Thus I began to frequent the dhikr circle that the shaykh held at his place every Monday evening. I never felt at ease with those visits, which I conducted secretly, not to be seen by one of my pals and become their laughingstock. We used to be around ten, sometimes more, people. They made me feel very welcome, taking pride that one of the educated young people had joined them, especially because, in the words of Shaykh Shaltut, a sea of blood and poison lay between the educated and religion. We would sit on a reed mat and concentrate our thoughts on God. Then we would begin to recite His name silently. Then out loud. Then we would sway to the rhythm of His name. Then fervor would impel us to stand up. And the coarse voices of the men would well up from their chests in a quavering lament declaring repentance and pleading for forgiveness, their quick breath converging into a single rhythmic, husky cry: Allah, Allah, Allah.

Suddenly I stopped going, having grasped that my absorption in dhikr would never lead me to a solution for the problem: it was up to me to find a solution if I were serious about it. Besides, I had come to notice something: Sultan Hamid could not be a holy man, because holy men are not called sultans but shaykhs. So, why was he 'Sultan' Hamid?

I wondered how such a simple clear fact had escaped my notice. How could I have not thought of that before? I began to find excuses for the people of our village that I had dismissed as fools for not asking questions about Sultan Hamid. Sometimes it was difficult, nay impossible, to think about things we got used not to thinking about; things that we are used to taking as they are: it is wrong to torture animals, but fine to slaughter them; women grew their hair but men cut it short; and a car owner is accorded more respect than a barefooted man though both are human beings. To begin reviewing one's belief in issues taken as given is not only difficult but well-nigh impossible.

4

had come to believe that if anyone was going to help me solve this mystery, it was going to be Ahmadi Effendi, who knew everything about everything. He must have an explanation of the story of the sultan who had a maqam while not being a holy man. Ahmadi Effendi was the first to don a suit and tarboosh in our village; the first to board a train and travel to Cairo; and the first not to work in the civil service but go directly into companies and banks. He was in his eighties and long retired. He came back to live in the village off the revenue of the few feddans he owned. We often came across him walking in the village, his upright figure unbent by age. Instead of the suit he now wore a spotless white gallabiya with one pocket on the chest. He held on, however, to his tarboosh and his chain watch, which extended from a buttonhole in the gallabiya to the chest pocket.

When we boys came across him on one of the streets, we would normally step aside politely and would not dare look him in the face except from a distance. His face had assumed, from long familiarity with the tarboosh, a serious, dignified look. He had a small mustache in which every hair appeared well groomed, while his lips were always tightly pursed together. His cheeks, on the other hand, were drawn in with no teeth left to support them. Everything in him was serious. He was serious when he talked, when he yelled, and when he joked too. And he never laughed except in conversation with the village head.

It was a real act of daring for me to go and ask him. It was not on for a young man like me to go speak to an elder effendi like him. That was another of our village's unquestionable conventions. Ahmadi Effendi bent down to place his ear with the dwindling hearing faculty near my mouth from which words were coming out stutteringly and almost inaudibly. Every time I asked a question, he would say, "What? What did you say?" and I would repeat it. Finally he appeared to hear me because he straightened his back again and leaned carefully on his handled walking stick, and stared at me with narrow dark eyes, which I felt, had they been mine, I would not see anything at all.

My awkwardness peaked, and my eyes were fixed on the chain of his watch, which I realized consisted of two branches joined together by an ornamental green crystal. He stared hard at me until I thought of leaving him standing and legging it home. But finally he said, "Well done, lad! Really clever of you to think of that. Whose son are you?"

My confusion redoubled as I explained to him where I came from and whose son I was.

"Why are you asking this question?" he said.

"In order to know," I said hesitantly as he asked me to repeat every word, "if he is a sultan or a holy man."

He turned his stick upside down so that the handle was on the ground, the bottom end up.

"Neither a holy man nor a sultan," he said, "don't believe this nonsense. What Sultan Hamid? I know Sultan Husayn, the late sultan of Egypt, God have mercy on his soul! I know Sultan Abd al-Hamid, the caliph of the Muslims; I know Sultan Ghuri, the greatest sultan of his day. But Sultan Hamid? Who is that? He doesn't even have a name fit for a sultan. He probably was some tramp. Holy man indeed! I've heard that he used to make charms for women that he would only give in a darkened room, while drunk. He would drink a whole bottle, a mix of half spirit and half vinegar, to be properly stoned. But I really am pleased with you. You seem a clever boy. My regards to your father. Say to him Ahmadi Effendi sends his greetings. So, what are you going to say to him?'

Ahmadi Effendi did not leave me on that day until he had tested me in Arabic, English, biology, and other school subjects, and had proven to me that our learning was not worth a nail clipping compared with that in his day. In the end he instructed me to banish from my mind that sultan story or he was going to protest to my father when he met him.

But I did not banish the matter from my mind. Rather it continued to bother me even more intensely, turning into an intractable problem. That stranger, who was not a holy man—why did the people of our village accord him so much honor? Why was a maqam built for him? And how did he gain such status in the hearts of people who did not know him? Was he a sultan? And if so, over what? Besides, the word 'sultan' is a big word, almost equivalent to the word 'king.' So, how can such a sultan be buried in our village, our little village known to nobody? And why particularly here? And how can a sultan's burial place be so modest?

5
_____

Given the enigmatic nature of the problem, it is surprising that sometimes I forgot it completely. The pattern was either to be completely immersed in it or to forget it completely. When I remembered it, I would vow not to concern myself with anything else for life; and when it slipped from my mind, its absence from my thoughts would be utter, as if I had never heard of the issue.

At first when I thought of the problem only to be defeated by it, I used to feel stifled, to want to kill myself. I was at the age when questions remaining unanswered was something unbearable. But frustration, carried to an extreme, backfires. So, I had begun to see the merits of our people's method. I was getting close to taking Sultan Hamid as a given, and not to worry about him any more than the people of our village. The thought of him nearly only occurred to me when I passed by the cemetery and glimpsed his maqam, gray and solitary in the distance, or if I got hold by chance of a piaster inscribed with the words, "minted during the reign of Sultan Husayn." Or again sometimes he would occur to me suddenly and without any trigger, as if our minds occasionally liked to ruminate what they held in storage, pushing it to the realm of consciousness for renewed sifting and thrashing.

But one day I made an astounding discovery that further complicated the issue. It so happened that the schoolboys of our village had a respectable soccer team. We had 'team 1' and 'team 2' and I was in neither. I was fond of the game but only as a spectator, and I often accompanied our team when it traveled to play against another village. They were genuine formal games with all arrangements documented and signed through correspondence between team managers. On the prescribed day (usually a Friday morning) the field would be lined, and satsumas and oranges bought for the halftime. Early in the morning old shoes would be sent to the shoemaker to fix, while the ball was sent to be filled with air and painted new with the juice of a tomato at the bicycle shop for a piaster. And we would be ready for the match.

That Friday we had gone to play against a village at some distance from our own. As usual the place chosen for the game by their team was near the village cemetery. It was rare to find in our villages a spacious and flat area suitable for a football game except in that space at the edge of the cemetery, also used as a granary in the threshing season.

A player of the other team kicked the ball so high, it flew past the pitch and the cemetery to land on top of a small stone building near the fields. I was taken aback to hear one of his mates shout at him, "Now who is going to get the ball from Sultan Hamid's roof?"

From that moment I was no longer able to follow the match, and as soon as it was halftime, I rushed to ask questions of the team we were playing. From their curt breathless words I learned that their village had another sultan by the name Hamid, who had a maqam very similar to that of our Sultan Hamid, also with a window from which white wax streamed down to freeze into rivulets and pools on the ground. He too was offered pledges, called upon for succor, and had prices discounted by vendors on the invocation of his name.

Before long I discovered through other matches in other places, and through inquiries here and there when there were no matches, that there were other sultans, that almost every village in our part of the country had its own Sultan Hamid. That was more than my mind, nay, more than all the minds in my village, could tackle. Yet, I did not leave a human being in my village or any other without engaging with them on this issue. What almost drove me crazy was the calm with which they took the matter, the way they were able to eat, drink, and sleep the night after hearing my questions. As if it were natural that every village have a sultan with the same name of Hamid. A private sultan with a private maqam. A sultan that no one knew how he came to be buried there, nor who built him the maqam. A sultan descended from outer space that they woke one morning to find his maqam standing at the edge of their cemetery, and his memory cherished in their hearts.

All I got were mysterious answers that added to my agitation, my feeling of inadequacy, and my anger. Someone would say it all happened a long time ago and no one knew the true story. Another would say he was a sultan related to the legendary hero, Abu Zayd al-Hilali Salama. Another still would argue that it was only one real sultan but that he had ordained in his will that tombs be erected for him in many places for his enemies never to be able to find his corpse. But someone else would posit that all that confusion was the responsibility of the government, and the government alone.

"What religion was he? What sect?" I would ask.

"God alone knows," would come the answer.

"Why do you love him so much? Why do you revere him and make vows in his name?" I would ask again.

"Who knows? It may be a wisdom beyond human understanding," again would come the answer.

I lost weight and began to see things and talk to myself. One day I looked in the mirror and nearly did not recognize myself. I was alarmed and I cursed the sultan and his secret and the very day I made him an offering of those candles. I feared I would die and I swore never to think of him again. My father made me swear in front of him in the hope my health would come back. But my health did not come back because I could not stop myself thinking about him.

My father took me to the doctor.

"What's wrong with you, son?" said the kind fat man as he took my lean hand in his soft, warm, and plump hand.

I was afraid he might consider me crazy if I told him and send me to a madhouse.

"Nothing!" I said.

He examined me and indeed found nothing.

But I was afraid I would lose my mind if I did not tell him. So, I took the opportunity of my father going out of the room and asked him hesitantly if he had an answer to the riddle that tormented me. I told him the full story and ended by saying that what made me sick was the failure to find an answer.

The doctor looked down with his chubby face until his double chin flattened. When he raised his head, I saw no derision in his look. All he did was raise his hand in front of my face.

"What are these, son?" he said moving his spread fingers and looking serious but benevolent.

"Your fingers," I said.

"How many are they?"

"Five!"

"Are you sure? Count again!"

Although I was of course sure, I actually counted them again and found them indeed to be five.

"Can you solve this riddle for me?" the man said smiling, "Why only five fingers in a hand? Why not three or six? Why just five? Answer me!"

I was not able to answer him, and meanwhile my father had returned to the room. The doctor saw us off to the door.

"Listen my son!" he began putting his five-fingered hand on my shoulder, "In this world there are many things without explanation. Why should you pick Sultan Hamid's story to make it the cause of your death? In order to find a solution for it, you must think; in order to think, you must live; and in order to live, you must eat. Eat!"

I ate and ate until I stopped thinking, and until my body grew and I became an adult. I left schools and joined others, and I forgot everything about the sultan, as we tend to do, when in our adulthood we forget all that worried us when young.

6

After many, many years, I was on holiday in the village one summer. One evening I came back home to find a stranger sitting in the house courtyard eating dinner in a fast, uncouth manner. The man's presence did not surprise me. I concluded that he must be one of my great-grandfather's peculiar guests. My great-grandfather, despite all those years, was still an old man as he used to be, and still pursuing his two favorite hobbies: drinking sweet coffee surreptitiously and hosting strangers. That latter hobby of his was driven by a passion for conversation. He found great pleasure in telling stories to anyone who listened, or to listen himself to someone telling a story. He was disenchanted with our village because there was no one in it any longer who knew how to tell a story: all the good raconteurs, he thought, were long dead and buried, leaving behind a generation that, like muzzled animals, was unable to speak. Rare as that was, my grandfather was drawn to any stranger who arrived in our village.

No one was happier than he when, after the evening prayer at the mosque of an evening, he noticed a stranger

161

among the rows of worshipers, for it was the custom of strangers when they arrived in a village to make their way to the village mosque, where the chances of being hosted were highest, and where they would be able to spend the night if no one extended his hospitality. No sooner did my great-grandfather notice the stranger than he dragged him by the hand to our house. This was by no means unproblematic for the household, but in the end he would have his way: the kitchen would swing into action, the guest would be fed, coffee would be slow-brewed, and my great-grandfather would lean on two cushions and bring out the tobacco tin and begin to chew on the leaves which he had spent hours during the day pounding in the mortar and seasoning with spices. My great-grandfather would spare no effort in accommodating his guests' most particular preferences: cigarettes if he was a smoker, or even shisha if he preferred to draw at moist honeyed tobacco. And then conversation would begin.

Those visitors who dropped in on our village had strange stories behind them. They did not normally visit for any particular reason. They were odd kinds of people who went around villages and spent a night in each. Most of them had no trade: they were just aimless wanderers. Some were repentant robbers; others jobless workers from the city; and some just unhinged in the head. Many were farmers bankrupted by that hard business but who had found no other job. What was common to all of them was that behind each was a story, a frightful bloody story: husbands cheated on by wives who turned them out of the house after stripping them of all they possessed; individuals who said they were destined to wander God's land until the end of their days; and others in whose eyes you saw a restless lost gaze, the gaze of a stray dog, the gaze of one who had no family, no home, no one to be concerned about him, and who knew not where he was going and cared nothing whether the sun rose ever again.

I must have inherited that hobby from my elder, for my greatest pleasure, me too, was to sit next to my great-grandfather on such occasions, and then no force on earth would be able to wrench me from my place or stop me from listening to the stranger's stories, watching his every movement and expression.

That night I sat staring at the new stranger. He was wearing an old garment and a red turban with a black patch at the back. His appearance did not suggest perplexity or madness. Only his eyes were constantly shut; he only opened them when he spoke, shutting them again at once as soon as he finished talking.

My great-grandfather had a charming manner in making people feel at ease and start talking. He would keep quiet until the stranger had finished eating, drunk his tea or coffee, and had a few puffs of tobacco. Often that was all that was needed for the man to start talking of his own accord without need for prodding. Most of those strangers did not exaggerate or lie when they talked, as if they realized it was one night, no more, and that their listener was a road companion and nothing more, and no matter how splendorous hyperbole and mendacity might be, the most wonderful thing for a man was to be able, if only once, to say the truth without it causing him trouble.

The man said that he was from Fayoum; that he was on his way to Syria as a token of his love for God; that he had been walking for fifty days, and had another hundred days' walk ahead of him. He was not entertaining, and had the manner of speaking then falling silent and closing his eyes before finishing what he was saying.

My great-grandfather began to yawn, and I was not allowed to talk, having been warned a thousand times not to utter a word if someone was talking: I was only allowed to sit and listen. Often the speaker would fall silent, and the silence would go on while the fire turned into cinders, and the cinders became enveloped in a thin layer of ashes. Meanwhile outside the night too would be silent, while the croaking frogs filled the night with a bass rhythmic tune, as if it were the snoring of the earth, fallen into deep slumber.

In one of the long silence intervals, I let out the question which had bothered me for hours. "Why the red turban with the black patch at the back?" I asked.

"That's how we dress," he replied.

At this point my grandfather straightened himself and shook sleep off.

"Which order do you belong to," he asked, "and who dresses like this?"

"We are not an order," answered the man, opening his eyes, "We are the sons of Sultan Hamid; we are not an order."

At first his answer sounded so banal requiring not the least comment, but the next moment I was shaking with excitement. I got up on my knees, grabbed the man by his hands, and beseeched him to tell me all he knew about the sultan.

The man listened to me while fixing his gaze in my direction from behind his closed eyes. He remained motionless for so long, but eventually he raised his head and confronted me. His eyes were red but he was not crying.

"Why do you attack the sultan like this?" he screamed suddenly at me.

I explained quietly that I was only asking, not attacking.

"What have you got to do with him?" he continued irately. "Why don't you mind your own business and leave people alone?"

I drew back.

"He's done nothing wrong," my great-grandfather interposed, "he's only asking—what's wrong with asking? Tell him!"

Suddenly the man fell silent and his head dropped on his chest.

"Yes. I will tell him. I will tell him about my beloved sultan," he said in a wail as if blaming himself, "He was a blessed man, my son."

"What do you mean, 'blessed'"? I said excitedly, "Did he perform miracles?"

"Blessed! Don't you know the meaning of 'blessed'"? he said. "What use is your education then? The one who scattered the enemy—wouldn't he be blessed? The one who defeated the infidels—wouldn't he be blessed?"

"Who was that enemy?" I said, breathless.

"You don't know the enemy?" he shouted. "Is there anyone who doesn't know the enemy? He was the one with far-reaching power and he was the one who defeated them. Help, O powerful one! Help! O Sultan Hamid, Conqueror of the infidels! Help! My beloved Sultan! Help! O help!"

His voice had reached the pitch of a muezzin calling for prayer.

"Help! O Sultan of far-reaching power!" he went on, his big larynx rising and falling in his long neck, "Help! O one with the many maqamat in Cairo, in Sohag, in Ashmon, and in all the land. People have only one maqam but you have a thousand. Help! O loved one!'

We did not dare interrupt him as he was swept over by a spiritual tide. It was clear he was not ranting; he appeared genuine and his crying was real.

When he calmed down and I felt safe that he was not going to flare up again, I began to ask him questions again. To my surprise he started to talk, his voice remorseful, like one who had given in. But his story did not satisfy me. What he said was something like the following:

When the invading enemy attacked Egypt, Sultan Hamid and his companions stood against them and he said to them, "By God, you will only enter over my dead body." When the enemy saw that he was wearing a gallabiya, they thought little of him. When one of them went up to him and raised his sword, Sultan Hamid snatched the sword from him and twisted it. The enemy tried to push him from his spot, but they soon realized it would be easier to move a mountain from its place. Ten of the enemy tried to push him aside but they could not. Their general looked and saw that his feet were dug in the ground and his head up in the sky. Sultan Hamid said, "By God, if you brought a thousand more armies like yours, all the armies of the world will not be able to make me budge from the land." They kept thinking about how to defeat their opponent. Suddenly an old man from among them leapt to his feet and said, "I've found it, friends. I know how we can beat him. This man's body is pure. No sword can hurt him as long as he remains pure. Only if he is made impure can a weapon pierce him." They asked him how that was to be done. "Leave it to me," he said, "I'm going to urinate on his legs to defile him, and you must strike him with your swords then." The filthy old man stood and urinated on the sultan's leg and from behind him came a treacherous sword that with one swing sent the leg flying. Our sultan said to them, "So what? A leg is gone, but I have another." And he took one step back. In the same manner they cut off his other leg. He laughed and said, "I still have hands. I swear to God, infidel enemies, I will show you, I will scatter you." The filthy old man kept urinating and after him the swords kept slashing the sultan's immaculate body in every village where fighting took place. What the enemy did not realize was that every piece of flesh severed would grow into a man to fight the infidels, saying, "I am the son of our father, Hamid. I am the sultan. I will show you the stars in broad daylight." They cut him into a million pieces, and every piece became a man. By the time they reached his head, they were already in Syria, and his sons had multiplied into many thousands, who charged the enemy, every one of them picking up an infidel, lifting him above his head, and hurling him into the bottom of the sea. When the enemy was exterminated and the land was clean of them, the sultan said, "Praise be to you, Lord!" and gave up the ghost on the spot.

At this point the stranger fell asleep suddenly. His head fell on his chest and his snoring rose without warning.

I was replaying his story in my head and trying to figure out historically who the "enemy" could have been, when I saw the man's head in the red turban rise suddenly and heard him say as if talking in his sleep, "Say God is one! Leave things be! God will provide. He who sows good deeds will never reap treachery. People do not forget: be kind to them on Saturday, they will pay you back on Sunday. All for the sake of the sultan. Help, O Sultan! Help O loved one!"

7

During all the years that I kept eating and growing, having shelved the sultan's issue, I had not in truth despaired of finding a solution. In fact, I was still being driven by a vague hope. But when the good-hearted doctor showed me his fingers and asked me that question, I lost sight of my hope, but only for a period.

The story of my great-grandfather's weird Sufi visitor was by no means rational. It certainly did not have the respectability of the doctor's words to me. But life can be very strange. For out of the blue I found that things that had long been suppressed in my chest eased and their weight lifted. My soul opened up and I felt relieved. I felt that I only had to stretch my hand and a solution for the problem of the sultan would be found.

Something had happened since I listened to the ravings of the stranger. It was as if I had doubted the existence of God and been tormented by the matter for a long time, then suddenly I found an extraordinary telescope through which I could look at the sky and ascertain the existence of God.

I did not dismiss the Sufi's ravings as just that but took them from a different angle. I thought Sultan Hamid must have been a man who lived and died as people did. But what a life he must have led! What a man he must have been! I wondered what he must have done to be held in such awesome reverence by people, for people to lose their wits in his love and become his followers for generations, for legends to be woven around his name, and for hundreds of maqamat in hundreds of villages to be erected for him and for scores of candles to be lit for him every night, year in, year out, maybe for hundreds of years.

And there was something else. To do something good is a matter between you and yourself. But for people to appreciate your deeds and therefore your person is another matter. The world is full of good people who lived and died for others—why are they not all appreciated? Why some and not others? On what basis do millions of people choose what to appreciate and what not? And why do some individuals become an object of adulation for the masses when they are not the noblest, the kindest, the most loving or the most self-sacrificial? I had no idea when I was turning those questions over in my head that I was going to find the answer for them with Roger Clément.

I had returned to Cairo from my short break at the village all excited not just about Sultan Hamid but the whole of life. I had been quite wrong, I came to realize, to spend so much of my life thinking about nothing but

171

the question of Sultan Hamid. As they say, you could find
what you are thinking about in what you are not thinking
about and vice versa.

That adage must be true, if only to the extent that
would make me believe that my encounter with Madam
International was beneficial. And by the way, her name
was not 'International'—she was called Jean and to this
day I don't know her nationality. Sometimes she said she
was Dutch. But her passport was from Luxembourg, and
she lived in Paris, according to herself. When I met her
she had just returned from South Africa on her way to
meet her Czech husband who was a mining engineer in
Poland. She herself found nothing odd about that. She
simply shrugged her shoulders and said, "I'm international." As to how I came to know her, it was very simple.
It was pure chance that made me visit Ismailia following
the Suez Crisis and the Tripartite Aggression on Egypt,
and pure chance that led me to bump into one of my
doctor friends in the dining room of the hotel I was staying. Again it was pure chance that made me accept a
generous offer from my friend to leave the hotel and go
stay with him in his room at the Ismailia Hospital where
he was a resident doctor. I loved the atmosphere of hospitals, the nurses in their white uniforms, and the gentle
smell of antiseptic wafting to my nose from a distance.

It was as a patient of the hospital that I got to know
Madam International. She was a passenger of the
Swedish ocean liner, the *Carolina*, stuck in the Suez
Canal as a result of the Anglo-French invasion. She was

incredibly crazy, that Jean. She was not really ill, at least not physically. She had tried to commit suicide on the ship and although she was saved right away, she claimed they came late after the aspirin she had taken had already circulated in her body, and that if she did not have a cardiogram without delay, her heart was going to stop at once. As the ship did not have a cardiograph, it was not difficult to guess Madam International's goal: to disembark from the trapped ship and stay on land. She had visited thirty-nine countries around the world and wanted to make the number forty so she could later tell her friends in Paris about the latest addition.

"Aren't you going to join your husband in Poland?" I asked her.

"No. We are going to meet in Paris." she answered, "I can only live in Paris."

"Why can't you have a goal for your life?" I asked her on another occasion.

"How can I when my goal in life is to live without thinking?" was her reply.

Had she not said that in her affected manner, I would have thought her a philosopher. Because of her, my doctor friend was barely able to rest in his room day or night during the three days that I stayed in the hospital. Hardly a few minutes would pass without him being disturbed on her account. He would be called because the 'foreign woman' was suffering from colic, but when he went to see her, he would find neither colic nor diarrhea. No sooner would he be back than there would be another knock on the door: the 'foreign woman' had urinary retention, and so on and so forth.

Often I joined my friend when he went to see her. He never got fed up with her. She was something new in his monotonous life and that of the whole hospital. I spent much time talking to her and often our conversations took us far, beyond the hospital walls and the tragic war. On one occasion I made the mistake of telling her the story of Sultan Hamid. It was as if all her life she had been waiting for someone to tell her a story like that. From that point on until she was practically wrenched out of her bed to return to the ship, she was still asking me questions, insistently, and probing this or that point, or being horrified at some detail, saying, "Incredible! Ya salam!" (The only phrase she learned from her days at the hospital.) She did not make do with my written address that I gave her but kept repeating it until she learned it by heart. "I will definitely write to you," she said as she was bidding me farewell. But I never believed she would.

I went back to my work in Cairo, and to the regular daily hours I spent at the national library, Dar al-Kutub. I was given a clue, and my visits to the library were to follow it up. I researched the names of all the sultans that ruled Egypt, or came to it as conquerors or visitors. I even looked into all the names of the Ottoman sultans. But there was not a single reference to a sultan by the name Hamid.

Thus came to an end this line of investigation, uncertain from the start. Every trace of the sultan was now lost.

But my enthusiasm did not wane. Twice a week I would go to the university library and the history department in the faculty of arts. It would be wrong to say that my efforts were in vain. During a few months I learned things about our history that I never dreamed of knowing. I also made a few friendships, not least that of Ali Bey, a dwarf of a height not exceeding a meter, who sold books walking between the Ataba and Azhar districts. By that time, the story of Sultan Hamid had leaked from me to my friends and their own circles. So much so, that sometimes I came across people I did not know who would smile at me and ask me, "Any news about the sultan?"

It was the same question that I heard from the youths of our village and even its older residents. And although the situation was reversed and the asking child had become the adult being asked, the answer I gave hardly differed from the ones that drove me mad as a child.

Many people volunteered ideas and suggestions. Sometimes someone would pat me on the shoulder saying, "I've found for you a book that might be useful." Another time, someone would hug me, "Done!" he would say, "I have unraveled the sultan's story." But when he began to speak, it turned out to be a different sultan. But I had expected anything except to open my letterbox one day to find a letter lying in the bottom with a foreign stamp on it. It was from Madam International.

As soon as I cut open the envelope, something dropped out of it, but I was not bothered and just went on to read the letter. I did not expect her to have such beautiful handwriting. I must also confess that as soon as I realized the letter was from her, images of her raced in my head and I felt I really missed her: a wearisome person can be attractive from a distance.

Unlike her affected manner of speech face to face that made you think she was playing a choreographed part rather than spontaneously talking to you, her writing style was so sober I thought she had been widowed. Most strange of all, she was writing about the sultan. She said that since the ship resumed its voyage out of the Suez Canal, she had thought of nothing save the issue of the sultan; that for the first time (and I'm quoting her directly) she felt there was something worth thinking about, no matter how much I might want to laugh at her; and that the result of her efforts was enclosed with the letter. I remembered the thing that had fallen out of the envelope: they were a few pages from a book.

I continued to read that amazing letter:

Don't ask how I have arrived at this result! For since my return to Paris, my friends and I have not rested for a moment and have had nothing to occupy us except the problem of Sultan Hamid. I wanted to tell you in detail about the tremendous efforts we put into this matter, but I think I will go straight to the most important issue. Last month saw the publication here of a book that has brought to light important historical documents. It consists of a collection of letters received by Monsieur Guy de Rouen from his friend Roger Clément, who was one of the archaeologists who accompanied Napoleon in his Egyptian campaign. It is thought that he did not return to France but became an Egyptian, wore the national dress and lived in Egypt. I am enclosing with this letter a few pages, taken from the book, which contain Roger's last letter. And for your information the book was edited and annotated by Dr. S. Martin, member of the Académie Française. This should reassure you as to the soundness of its contents. I do not know whether the account in the letter of the French archaeologist will be sufficient to solve the mystery of Sultan Hamid, but now you must read the thing for which you have waited for so long: I know you can't wait!

Please write and tell me about everything.

Yours,

Jean International

PS. Do you really have a village called Châteauneuf? Does it still exist? Please describe it for me in your reply.

8

The truth is I was anything but eager to read those pages. I was in a state more akin to shock; shock not caused by the stunning news but by feelings of reassurance. For I had never divulged to anyone that I had ideas similar to what the letter had already alluded to, but I had in fact often thought along those lines. Sometimes I was seized by an ambiguous fear; a concern that I might have blown up the matter more than the facts warranted. I was terrified that in the end I might discover that the so-called Sultan Hamid had no mystery, no problem; that it was I who created the mystery and fabricated the problem. If that had happened, I would probably have gone out of my mind.

At that moment I experienced a strange sense of serenity; serenity so profound, I was not motivated to move or pick up the papers that contained the solution. It was enough for me for the moment just to glory in the knowledge that there *was* a mystery.

I thought of Shatanof, or as she called it, Châteauneuf. Why had I forgotten that my great-grandfather had often talked to me about it? He told me that we had relatives there and that my great-great-grandfather left it during the days of drought and settled in our village. Why couldn't Sultan Hamid have lived for a period in Shatanof in the old days? Why couldn't I be one of his descendants?

Finally I thought I would have mercy on myself and read the extract from the book. But it was in French, which I only knew superficially, so I hastened with the papers to a friend of mine, well-versed in the language, and we collaborated in translating the text, consisting of a letter preceded by a note from the contemporary editor of the collection, as follows.

Letter no. 10

This is the last letter in the collection. However, a different school of thought believes that Monsieur Clément did send a later letter to his friend, Monsieur de Rouen, but that the latter tore it up after reading it for reasons as yet unknown.

As for what happened to Roger Clément after sending this letter, that remains beset with uncertainty. Some researchers assert that he came back to France toward the end of his life, where he died. Personally, I am not of this view.
What follows is the text of the letter.

Cairo, 20 June 1801
Dear Guy,
I still do not know if my last letter has reached you or gone astray. Nor do I know if you have written a

reply which also has gone astray. Or maybe I am just too distrustful of our respectable postal service.

Anyway, whether this letter met the same fate as the one before it or reached you safely, I feel I must write to you, even if I were sure it wasn't going to reach you, because there are so many things taking place inside me that I want to unburden to a friend. As you know, I wouldn't dare to whisper to anyone here what goes on in my mind. I know you will laugh at me as you usually do, but please try to understand me because people here do not want to.

In your letter of six months ago you asked me to tell you about Egypt and the Egyptians—those people who live on the banks of the Nile. Well, dear friend, those people are my problem.

I admit that I was not the way I am now when I first arrived here. You know France is my life, and I have done my share in advancing the Republic. And when I set foot in Egypt, I thought I was landing in a dark African country to which I was bringing the flame of civilization and the glories of the Republic enjoyed by my own country. But today, I am—what shall I say? I have witnessed supernatural powers with my own eyes, Rouen. I have been touched by their magic—but you will not understand. No one in the world—your world—will understand what I mean. Why should I exercise my pen and hand to no avail?

All right! I will act like a tour guide and tell you about Egypt. I think it is this that you want to hear about. Egyptians, my friend, are not like what you think. They do not dance around fire at night, and their women have nothing to do with the harem of *The Thousand and One Nights*. The Egyptians, unlike what you might think, are not the Mamluks. We finished with those in our first round with them. They arrived in a long line wearing loose silken garments and mounting graceful horses, behind each of them a black slave running. They came in the manner of Don Quixote, swords drawn, taunting us to step out for duel.

The General's [*Napoleon*] response was decisive: he ordered his artillery to fire on them on the spot. They fell in their hordes cursing the cowardice of the French. In one or two battles we were finished with them, as I said.

As for Egyptians, some live in Cairo and other cities but most work at tilling the land and live in black villages in the countryside, the color of the mud of which they are built; they are called the fellahin. An unfathomable breed, those fellahin, Guy!

When you see them at close quarters, their faces smiling to you kindly, naively, and you realize their instinctive shyness of strangers—you might be tempted to think little of them; you might be forgiven if you thought that if you slapped one of them on the back of his neck, he would not dare look up at you and would walk away submissively swallowing the insult. But do not make that mistake,

181

Guy! Napoleon, Kléber, and Billot—they all tried and lived to regret it.

No one can fathom the depths of those people—that tribe with homogeneous features that descended into the Valley of the Nile a long time ago, vowing never to budge or fragment; that tribe who learned to bend before the storms of invaders, only to chew on them slowly later; that tribe who live in a valley open to invasion from all directions with the smallest of armies. But the problem does not lie in invasion. It is what happens after invasion that is the problem.

I challenge history itself to produce a single invader who conquered these lands and was able to leave unscathed. They have a strange tool, those peasants, which they use to grind grain. It is made of a huge round stone placed on top of another. The grain is fed whole through a hole in the top stone to come out from between the two stones fine flour. The Turks here have turned into fine flour a long time ago; the Mamluks were on their way. I do not know where the Egyptians' strength lies, nor how this process takes place. But take place it does.

I am not going to claim that the story of Hamid illustrates what I want to say. But you can have a go at interpreting it, if you can. I have come to this land as an enemy. I will not kid myself into saying, as they all do here, that I came to liberate the Egyptians from the rule of the Mamluks. I came as an enemy, my friend. We all came as a strong enemy armed with the latest weapons of destruction invented by Europe. We came as powerful invaders, but today we are in a crisis. Our problem now is how to wrench our legs out of the mire of this country to save ourselves from those people before we melt into them and disappear.

I will not pretend that I can speak informatively about the Egyptians: I can do no such thing. I will only tell you about Hamid. For months he has been our favorite subject of conversation, when we can have conversation. Suffice it to say the general command has issued an unwritten order not to talk about him.

This Hamid is not an Egyptian leader. In fact, until a few months ago nobody cared for that Hamid or thought much of him. He was a mere fellah of the village of Châteauneuf situated between the two branches of the Nile. You might wonder about this French name for an Egyptian village. The fact is the original name of the village was Kafr Shindi, and next to it was an old Mamluk castle. When we conquered the Delta and expelled the Mamluks, we demolished the old castle and built a new one with local materials and called it Châteauneuf [*the new castle*]. We also renamed the village after the name of the castle. And do not think I am being sarcastic when I say that that was all our mission toward Africa's dark countries had come to: substituting a name for another. But the fellahin adapted our change to suit themselves: they call the village Shatanof, instead of Châteauneuf.

Billot's policy since taking charge of the castle was to avoid harassing the fellahin in order to safeguard the security of the castle, and not because we were the friends of the Egyptians, as the good man was trying to get the fellahin to believe. In fact it was the policy of the French army at large to try to make friends with the native population and strengthen ties with them.

But this policy benefited us nothing. Every time we tried to get closer to them, they recoiled farther from us. Whenever we tried to convince them that we had saved them from the Mamluks' tyranny, they would stare hard at us, as if saying, "You came to save us from the Mamluks, the Mamluks came to save us from the Turks, the Turks came to save us from the Tartars, the Tartars came to save us from the caliph, the caliph came to save us from the Ptolemies, and the Ptolemies came to save us from the Greeks—why do you favor us with your gallantry, gentlemen?"

And how cruel the gaze of an Egyptian when it falls on a foreign enemy! Among themselves they treat each other like rival cockerels. All day they trade insults. One's father can be reduced to any of a range of a hundred titles that begin with a slipper and expand to encompass the full gamut of footwear, not to mention the animal kingdom down to swine. Furthermore, any organ of a mother's body can become suitable material for hurling insults. This is a nation whose wealth of insults is unmatched by any other, and when they talk, they can only do so in shouting. Yet, let a stranger—any stranger—try to lay a hand on one of them! A miracle would immediately happen: they would all turn on the stranger, having forgotten their differences and recriminations.

We always felt the heat of their gaze. How cruel to live among people who do not try to hide their hostility! Thus the gulf between us continued to widen until the Cairo rebellion that I have told you about before. Since that eruption, our soldiers' nerves were ever so taut. Thus despite Billot's instructions and daily reminders, one of our soldiers camped in Châteauneuf lost his nerve one day and shot and killed a fellah who was following him with his gaze.

The incident had a devastating effect on the village. The angry fellahin led by the village head went to meet Colonel Billot, who wasted no time and came to meet them at the gate. They demanded that the murderer be executed in front of them. Billot tried to assure them that the murderer would be tried and punished, but they were adamant that he choose between two things: either to execute the murderer or to hand him to them to punish him. Billot rejected both propositions and ordered them to leave.

They obeyed and left. But the following day, one of the soldiers was killed on his way back to the castle. Billot led a large force to the village and arrested the village head and brought him to the castle. A crier went around the village announcing that unless the killer turned himself in before sunset, the village head was going to be executed by firing squad.

Before sunset, a fellah turned up at the castle declaring himself to be the killer and demanding the release of the village head. Billot took the whole matter simply and decided to hang the fellah after trying him in front of the village to make an example of him. That was the worst decision of his life.

On the following day the accused was taken to the main square of the village. All villagers were driven to the square to witness the trial. The court consisted of Billot in the chair, and Major Lasalle and Sergeant Jean Berget, members. There was also a prosecutor. And as for the defense, to your surprise I am sure, I undertook that myself. I had arrived on that day to spend a few days as a guest of Billot and to study the life of the fellahin at close quarters.

All I was told about the defendant was his name, Hamid. He did not seem to me any different from the rest of the fellahin in appearance, except for being tall and having a long nose and big eyes. His little finger on the left hand was missing, as I noticed. On each of his cheeks there was a tattoo of a sparrow (to strengthen his eyesight, as the dragoman told me). Naturally, I did not want to take part in that comic show, but my friend, Billot, put pressure on me to do my 'duty,' especially as I was the only one present with a doctorate in law.

And of course it was a travesty. The fellahin were sitting or standing in the square casting at us glances that, like their language, we did not understand. Meanwhile, the court exchanged sarcastic remarks in loud voices, and none of this was helped by a clumsy interpreter who hardly knew Arabic, or for that matter, French.

My turn came to make the case for the defense. I do not know what Billot thought of my defense, which I started with reference to the French Revolution and its sacred mottos of liberty, fraternity, and equality. How ironic it was to utter those words in the square of Châteauneuf, when the sentence had been passed a priori and only waited to be carried out.

Fortunately, or maybe unfortunately, I was not able to complete my defense. They attacked us. We did not know where they came from, but the square was filled with cudgel-waving hands, and the savage blood-curdling cries of "Lahakbar, lahakbar!" I cannot describe to you the terror that seized us—court, prosecution, defense, and guards. We were still suffering from the 'fellahophobia' that had befallen us. For it so happened that after seizing Cairo, Napoleon sent an army led by Martin to occupy the eastern Delta. The army set out at dawn, only to return by noon in a pitiable state. The soldiers, their uniforms tattered, were trembling and in their eyes was a look of crazed terror. Each told a different story of savage people who fell on them with bludgeons, sticks, axes, scythes, thundering cries of "Lahakbar, lahakbar!" (which means "God is greater than all"). As you know, our soldiers are the elite of the French army; the elite with whom our great leader, Napoleon, conquered Austria, Spain, and Poland, and achieved victory in Salzburg and Italy; the elite that scattered the strong and brave Mamluks in two battles. Can you imagine such an elite force, armed with rifles and guns, running away in consternation from a crowd with no weaponry but sticks and scythes? Running away without firing a shot or trying to regroup? And why should I hide from you that some of our soldiers wet their pants with terror? No one was able to explain this phenomenon. Was it the sheer savagery of the fellahin assault? Or some unknown factor?

The incident had far-reaching results. The dramatic return of Martin's soldiers had a devastating effect on the morale of the entire army. Since that date our soldiers have been in terror of the fellahin to the extent that a doctor of the army coined a term to describe the condition: fellahophobia. However, this disorder disappeared gradually as we consolidated our conquest of Egypt. When we saw the Egyptians from close up, we did not find them to be man-eating savages. On the contrary, we found them to be kind and gentle, if shy of strangers. We found them obedient too, and sometimes naive. It was difficult to believe that those were the people who terrorized Martin's forces to the point of turning them into herds of frightened animals running wildly for safety.

No sooner did we see those bludgeons in the hands of the attacking fellahin than we raced to the castle to take shelter. There were no casualties on that day: we only lost the defendant. In the midst of the mayhem they managed to free him and take him away. Billot was mad with rage. He summoned all his soldiers to the castle court and harangued them with a speech full of rebuke. He vowed to lead them out of the castle and not return without Hamid and ten more fellahin. I left him in the middle of his endeavors and went back to my excavations in Cairo near the pyramids. The news of what happened after I had left reached us regularly from Cairo. Not just me; everybody knew.

Billot led his entire force out of the castle and laid siege to Châteauneuf. He searched all houses and all the fields around the village but did not find Hamid. Consequently he arrested the village head and ten others from the inhabitants. The crier announced that unless Hamid was delivered, they would be executed. The sun set without Hamid turning up. Billot was fearful that if he executed the captured fellahin, riots would escalate. Consequently he extended his notice to the village. When nothing happened, Billot was enraged. He had the village head shot but kept the others alive.

The news of the execution of the village head resonated in Châteauneuf and the surrounding villages, and a rumor circulated that the fellah Hamid had sworn to kill Billot in revenge for the village head. Billot, however, was not the kind of man to be frightened by threats. He continued to lead the patrols looking for Hamid, but on one occasion he came back on horseback, his body riddled with holes.

That night Napoleon did not sleep. He ordered the forces camped in Shabrakhit to be marched to Châteauneuf and put no lesser figure than General Kléber in charge. The new commander's task was to search Châteauneuf and the surrounding areas for that Hamid person, the fellah with the amputated little finger on the left hand and sparrow tattoos on his cheeks.

The purpose in seeking to arrest Hamid was not only to execute him but also to restore the name of our army. His capture became an end in itself because his murder of Billot had earned him huge popularity in neighboring villages. The feelings of the fellahin toward us as the foreign infidel enemy were beginning to crystallize around the person of that Hamid, not least because our army was not particularly courteous in seizing the villagers' food and horses without compensation.

Kléber conceived a foolproof plan: laying siege to the central Delta in its entirety. Everyone thought Hamid would be captured any day. But we were facing, my friend, strange people whom we did not understand. Kléber discovered that *he* was the one besieged by those look-alike people who understood each other but remained inscrutable to all others.

As I told you, the distinguishing marks of Hamid were the tattoo on his cheeks and his amputated little finger. Now, see what happened.

All cornfields were left without harvest: the cobs were picked leaving the stalks standing. That is because in Egypt's open flat land you can only hide in cornfields. In those fields you may be separated from a person by a few steps, but you will not see him. Kléber learned through his many spies that every village in the Delta had prepared a house and a wife for Hamid. Kléber would receive news that Hamid would be in such and such village on such and such day, and so a force would attack the village and encircle it tightly. Yet Hamid would slip from house to house until he reached the edge of the village to be swallowed by a cornfield.

Everyone found with two sparrow tattoos and an amputated little finger would immediately be arrested, but it was noticed that the number of those arrested was disproportionately increasing. On investigation it transpired that the fellahin—in order to protect Hamid—were rushing in their droves to have their cheeks tattooed and their little fingers amputated in order to make it impossible to distinguish the real Hamid. Thus sparrow tattoos on the cheeks, which were thought to be a way to strengthen eyesight, turned into a popular motif, while amputating little fingers became a competition among the men and youths of the villages and a mark of bravery and endurance.

What happened, my friend, was inevitable. Gradually small bands of men with sparrow tattoos and no little fingers on their left hands began to form and waylay and attack our forces and assassinate soldiers. The bandits called themselves "the Sons of Hamid." They called Hamid himself "Hamid the Great," and then "Hamid the Sultan"; this last title being a sign of superlative veneration. The name of Hamid became a source of grave perturbation for Kléber. Whenever our men marched through a village, its children would follow them, shouting, "Hamid! Hamid!" The muezzins who called people for prayer in the mosques (the human equivalent of church bells in France) would repeat at the end of the call, "Give me victory, O God!

over my enemies, for I am your *hamid*." When soldiers got them, they claimed to be only raising prayers to God. (Later I knew that they were punning on the name of Hamid, which also means "he who praises God.")

Arresting Hamid became a well-nigh impossible goal, and laying siege to the central Delta proved futile. The man had just melted into the rough mass of bodies belonging to those people we thought naive. Destroying the name of Hamid became more important than destroying him in person, that name which had turned into a magical charm, more fatal than all the rifles of our army. The fellahin just fired it at will at our soldiers whenever they saw them. They said it every day, every moment, without ceasing, making its effect on the soldiers' spirits worse than bullets. Often they lost nerve and burst out crying, or shot at their tormentors. For every one of them killed, one of us was killed.

Sultan Hamid's name was all over the Delta, then it came to Cairo and was all the rage among its inhabitants, even in Sufi rings where it was chanted in their rituals and called upon for support. Finally the name invaded Upper Egypt and bands of the Sons of Sultan Hamid were in every place. That name wreaked havoc on our nerves, my friend. The laborers I employed in my digs—when they spoke, they only said Hamid. They may have said other things, but in my ears I only heard *Hamid, Hamid.*

We reached a stage when we could no longer bear to hear that name. And how silly I thought their belief in that Hamid fellow was! In my view they were like children, who the more you try to take from them something they are holding, the more they cling to it.

But no matter how much I disdained them and their belief, deeper inside I admired them. Just imagine the way they adopted one word, Hamid, just one word, and turned it into a fearful force! Only because they believed in it, my friend. They are astonishing, those people—their belief does not arise from thought and reason, but love. They love to the point of faith. And they have an enormous power for love, my friend. The extent of their love for one another (despite the constant exchange of insults I have told you about) shows in the intricate family relations they have. For example, a certain Muhammad can be the son of the maternal cousin of Omar. And if you mention someone's name in front of one of them and he says to you, "Oh yes, he is a relative of mine," it is more likely than not that what he means is that a person from his village has married into the village of the person whose name you mentioned; nothing closer. They are not a group of people—those Egyptians: they are a mass. And that mass of theirs had completely formed around the person of Hamid until the general, Napoleon in all his power, appeared a dwarf next to him. Let me tell you what happened.

A few months ago our forces received a piece of news that made them dance in jubilation. It was the happiest news they had heard since the conquest of Egypt: Hamid was killed. It so happened that one of our officers who had been present at his trial was on patrol with a few soldiers when he glimpsed him in the market place. He shot him dead on the spot. Had he not managed to escape with his men in the confusion that gripped the place, the crowds would have torn them into pieces.

I will not tell you about the rage that swept Egypt from corner to corner or its shattering consequences. Suffice it to say that one outcome was that the castle of Châteauneuf was burned to the ground, and Cairo rose up in arms for the second time, while the Mamluks announced the independence of Upper Egypt. The situation was extremely dangerous, and in my dreams I often saw that we were all being slain by the roadside. We were living on the top of a volcano that we feared would any moment open its massive mouth and swallow us.

No sooner were we able to breathe again after all this turbulence following the assassination of Hamid, than more unexpected news reached us. The fellahin had not moved Hamid from the spot where he fell: he remained in his place, nobody touching him. Within three days they had built over him a shrine with a high dome.

195

What drove Kléber crazy was that people had started to visit the shrine in inestimable numbers. Every day they came and met around the shrine as armies of ants meet around a crumb of bread. Kléber went mad because he realized that the murder of Hamid had changed nothing. What happened was that Hamid had turned from a mere name circulating among people into a visible reality that has a place topped with a high dome. Try to imagine, my friend, how a person becomes in his death far more dangerous than he was in life! Try to picture masses of people coming from far-flung places for no reason but to visit the shrine of a dead man, even if his killer was a French soldier!

What had that Hamid done for them to gather around him in such a spectacular manner? Was it just because he killed a Frenchman to avenge the murder of a fellow fellah that they raised him to such pinnacles of reverence? Or was it because he acted at a time when people needed to see someone take action in order for them to be released from their shackles and rush in every direction?

"Do you love Sultan Hamid?" I asked one of the laborers who worked with me.

"More than my own children," he answered.

"Would you die for him?"

"Not once, but again and again."

"Why?"

"Why! That's not a question to ask."

"What do you know about him?"

"All I know is I won't hesitate to die for him."

"Who is Sultan Hamid, Muhammad?"

"It's enough that he died a martyr."

"Nothing else?"

"Nothing else?"

We conquered these people with our superiority, our guns, our brass music, our printing press, our chemistry—but where can we get their miraculous ability to turn into one mass, to love and survive? Where can we get the ability to be individuals when we want, and merge into one mass when we want? We may have amazed them with our civilization, but believe you me! They struck awe in me with their Hamid.

Poor General Kléber! The news of the thousands who visited the shrine made him anxious and caused him to take a lot of magnesium sulphates. All he had achieved by killing Sultan Hamid was to give the Egyptians a tangible object to gather around, and call his name in voices that resonated under the skies.

The Sons of Hamid were very active. People would come to visit the shrine, not knowing why they came. But they would leave fully informed about the war that took place between him and the infidels, his treacherous murder, and the necessity of revenge.

197

Kléber decided not to wait for the volcano to erupt. He attacked the shrine with a massive force and pulled it down. He then exhumed the corpse and had it dumped in the Nile.

No sooner had he returned to his barracks, than the corpse was recovered from the water by unknown means, a spot by the riverbank was chosen to rebury it, and work was begun to build another shrine over it. Within days they had finished building a shrine larger than the first one. Before the building was completed, its location had already become known to the masses of fellahin and city dwellers, who began to visit it in their thousands.

Kléber convened a meeting of his commanders-in-chief and told them that that superstition had to be destroyed before it destroyed them. They consulted for a long time over what to do. If it were not for Kléber being a Catholic, he probably would have agreed for the body to be cremated. But they found a compromise. Hamid's corpse was to be cut up into small pieces and scattered all over the country. Then let the Egyptians find another god to believe in, or another superstition to cling to.

At night—and they would not have been able to carry out something like that except under cover of dark—the republican army crept into the shrine of Sultan Hamid and stole the corpse. After cutting it up, groups of soldiers traveled up and down the country dumping its parts here and there. That night Kléber slept deeply. But only for that night. For the news started to come in that the Egyptians had begun to erect a shrine over every spot where a part of Sultan Hamid's was found.

Now, instead of one Sultan Hamid, Kléber's problem was with hundreds of sultan Hamids, each visited by thousands upon thousands of people, who gathered around their shrines and shook the heavens with the chanting of their names. The shrines also became foci for the activism of the Sons of Hamid.

And can you blame me that the matter of Sultan Hamid began to preoccupy me at that stage to the extent that I was impelled to substitute the native dress for my European clothing and go to visit one of the hundreds of shrines erected for him in order to understand this attachment to him by his fellow Egyptians and discover why they have raised him to that divine status?

That was what I did yesterday. Thursday, the shrine-visit day. The day when thousands arrive from the far corners of the land to meet at the maqam, tanned by the heat of the sun and covered in the dust from the fields. What I witnessed was astounding. Crowds like that of Judgement Day. Multitudes of men in their soiled white garments. Multitudes of women in their black attire. An abundance of lights. Torch lights. Street lights. And lights without a known source, as if generated from the closeness of people. Tambourines whose beat struck terror in the heart. Brows glistening with sweat. Inscrutable eyes staring. Hands waving. Thousands of throats calling huskily, beseechingly, imperatively, "O Lord Hamid!" One cry compacted of millions of cries emanating from the chests pressing against each other. An enormous cry that gathers above the shrine like a consecrated cloud of a luminous tune. Shimmering. Trembling. Expanding to the beat of the tambourines.

I realized that what mattered was not what was under the dome of the shrine. What mattered were the strong rough bodies that surrounded it. What mattered was the single cry rising from the thousands of hungry broad mouths. What mattered was the other side of the supernatural beast that unseated the hearts of our soldiers with one blow from his hand. What mattered was what those masses generated; what rose out of them, collected and fused together to crystallize and intermix with the light of torches and the lights of streets and the beats of tambourines and the swaying of bodies.

I stood there dazed, my friend. As if I saw that invisible energy hung between the earth and the sky. As if I saw in concrete the amalgamated will of the masses. As if I saw all the love that was in people condensed into one cry. As if those rough bodies, soiled with the mud of the fields, produced a matter loftier than their living bodies; loftier than life; the quintessence of life; the consolidation of all that is capable and powerful in it; the consolidation of all that is irresistible; the supreme supernatural power; the secret of life.

The shrine of Hamid was the focal point at which the volitions of people met and converged; the point at which the will to eternity concentrated and turned into a magical elixir for everlasting life. How can I describe what I saw? I stood there in trembling piety watching the crowds as they joined ranks to manufacture belief and then put their faith in it. The single cry rose from the single heart to turn, when it met with other cries, into something living and lofty which finds its way back into individual hearts, purifying them and nourishing in them the will to survive.

I felt, my friend, that I stood before an insuperable power. I really felt that. I felt it to the extent that I nearly prostrated myself before it to ask forgiveness. I felt the elixir pouring into my soul and the tremulous iridescent music filling my heart and merging with my inner self, making me feel for the first time in my life the grandeur of life; the splendor of being human and possessed of this miraculous power, the power to gather together in order to create out of our congregation something higher than the life of each of us.

You will not comprehend my suffering, Rouen. It will be impossible for you to comprehend it without living it yourself. My problem is that I have lived it. I write this letter to you from a room in the castle. From the window I can see our soldiers going through their physical training regimen, cleaning their rifles, receiving new ammunition, oiling cannons, and taking orders. I can also hear the bugler sounding the General's salute. How I pity our soldiers and their General. What use are rifles and bullets? To subjugate these people by killing some of them? What use is it to kill people who bring back to life their dead? What use is it to kill people who create out of a dead man hundreds of living ones?

I am afraid, Rouen. Since yesterday I have felt overwhelming forces drawing me toward these people, calling on me to discover their secret. I tell myself it is an academic interest. But do not believe me, because I do not believe myself. I am resisting ferociously: my culture, my legacy, my reason—all should prevent me from being drawn into their mass when it forms. But I am no longer myself. Last night has changed so many things inside me. I am frightened my resistance will cease. I am frightened that today or tomorrow I will secretly make my way to one of the hundreds of shrines of Sultan Hamid, the fellah with the amputated little finger in whose mockery of a trial I took part. I am frightened to death that I will do for him what I used to do for the Virgin Mary at our church—light a candle and place it next to those of the impoverished fellahin to brighten his tomb.

It may be that my candle will count for nothing among all the veneration that the sultan is accorded. It will be just one candle among the hundreds which have illuminated and will continue to illuminate his hundreds of shrines for hundreds of nights, and who knows? —maybe for hundreds of years. But do not be surprised if I do it today, tomorrow, or one imminent evening. I feel myself walking involuntarily toward that fate. I feel my resistance weakening, vanishing.

Help! Rouen.

Roger

TRANSLATOR'S AFTERWORD

T*ales of Encounter*, the title of this collection of three
novellas or long short stories by Yusuf Idris (1927–
91), does not reflect the Arabic title of anything
written by Yusuf Idris, nor have these three works been
published together under one title in Arabic. The details
of their original publication in Arabic are as follows:
"Madam Vienna" was first serialized in weekly install-
ments in the Cairo daily *al-Masa'* between 17 July 1959
and August 7 of the same year; it was later included in
the collection *al-'Askari al-aswad wa qisas ukhra* (The Black
Policeman and Other Stories), Cairo, 1962. "New York
80" was published in Cairo in 1980 by Maktabat Misr,
twenty-some years after "Madam Vienna." The volume
also included "Madam Vienna," retitled "Vienna 60."
"The Secret of His Power" ("Sirruhu al-bati'") first
appeared in the collection *Hadithat sharaf* (An Incident of
Honor), published in Cairo, 1958.

Written and published at different times of the
author's career, the novellas are nevertheless broadly
united in that they are all approaches to a common

theme, namely that of the east–west encounter. Hence the title of convenience chosen for this collection: *Tales of Encounter*. The interest of Arab authors generally, and writers of fiction particularly, in exploring this theme goes back at least to the 1920s and has continued ever since.

Traditionally, fictional treatments took the form of a journey from east to west, where the eastern male protagonist will fall in love with a western woman. The story of the encounter will then be used allegorically to explore the wider relationship between east and west, with the eastern male and western female normally standing for their respective cultures.

I have selected the three present works by Idris to translate and publish in one volume as the best, though by no means the only, instances of his contribution to the encounter tradition of fiction writing in Egyptian and other Arab fiction. In "Madam Vienna" and "New York 80," as the reader will see, Idris adheres to the representation of the theme through the metaphor of a sexual encounter between an Egyptian man and a western woman, while in "The Secret of his Power" he adopts a different approach.

It is worth drawing readers' attention to a connection between the stories of "Madam Vienna" and "New York 80" that Yusuf Idris himself was keen on pointing out. While "Madam Vienna" was first published in 1959, it is to be noted that when he wrote and published "New York 80" twenty years later, he included in the same volume "Madam Vienna" retitled as "Vienna 60," though without indicating the fact on the book cover or title page. Readers interested in a critical appraisal of the current and other relevant works by Idris can have recourse to my comprehensive study of the encounter theme in Arabic writing over a two-century period in my book, *Arab Representations of the Occident: East–West Encounters in Arabic Fiction* (London and New York: Routledge, 2006).

GLOSSARY

Abu-Zayd al-Hilali: legendary hero (with historical origins) of a medieval popular Arab epic that survived orally into the twentieth century

Asmahan: (1912–44) popular Syrian–Egyptian female singer of the first half of the twentieth century

dhikr circle: a Sufi practice in which men stand in a circle chanting the name of God

Fatiha: the opening sura, or chapter, of the Qur'an, often recited in memory of someone who has died

gallabiya: an ankle-length, long-sleeved robe; traditional Egyptian garment for men, especially in the countryside

al-Husayn: grandson of the Prophet Muhammad; a shrine believed to contain his remains is housed in a grand mosque in old Cairo

Khazindar Square: a once stylish square in downtown Cairo

kuttab: traditional pre-elementary school for teaching the Qur'an and the basics of reading and writing, now extinct in Egypt

Lahakbar: Roger's rendition of "Allahu akbar!" "God is greater!"—an invocation to God often shouted in times of distress. Although the comparison is cut short, the implication is 'God is greater [than all].'

maqam (pl. maqamat): a holy man's or saint's tomb or shrine, sometimes self-contained, but often housed within a mosque

al-Masa': the title of a Cairene evening newspaper

La Putain respectueuse: a play by the famous twentieth-century French author and philosopher Jean-Paul Sartre, rendered in English as *The Respectful Prostitute.* In Arabic the feminine adjective meaning 'respectful' is *muhtarima,* while 'respectable' is *muhtarama,* with a single vowel making the difference. But short vowels in Arabic are normally not indicated in writing, so it is easy for 'respectful prostitute' to be misread as 'respectable prostitute,' leading to the erroneous allusions to "respectable prostitute" in Idris's *New York 80.*

Qasr al-Aini, Munira, Madbah: neighborhoods of Cairo

Rayya and Sakina: two women who became notorious for abducting and murdering bejeweled women in Alexandria in the early twentieth century. Their names have survived in the language and national consciousness as synonymous with horror.

al-Sayyida Zaynab: a neighborhood in central Cairo, named after al-Sayyida Zaynab, granddaughter of the Prophet Muhammad. She is believed to be buried in the grand mosque in the area bearing her name.

Shamm al-Nasim: an ancient Egyptian spring festivity, still observed in Egypt

shisha: the Egyptian word for narghile or water pipe

"*Tous les bateaux* . . .": two schoolbook sentences in French: "All the boats from every country are anchored in the port" and "Ali Kamil is a bright high-school student."

"Ya salam!": an exclamation of amazement

Betool Khedairi *Absent*
Mohammed Khudayyir *Basrayatha*
Ibrahim al-Koni *Anubis • Gold Dust • The Puppet • The Seven Veils of Seth*
Naguib Mahfouz *Adrift on the Nile • Akhenaten: Dweller in Truth*
Arabian Nights and Days • Autumn Quail • Before the Throne • The Beggar
The Beginning and the End • Cairo Modern • The Cairo Trilogy: Palace Walk
Palace of Desire • Sugar Street • Children of the Alley • The Coffeehouse
The Day the Leader Was Killed • The Dreams • Dreams of Departure
Echoes of an Autobiography • The Essential Naguib Mahfouz • The Final Hour
The Harafish • Heart of the Night • In the Time of Love
The Journey of Ibn Fattouma • Karnak Cafe • Khan al-Khalili • Khufu's Wisdom
Life's Wisdom • Love in the Rain • Midaq Alley • The Mirage • Miramar • Mirrors
Morning and Evening Talk • Naguib Mahfouz at Sidi Gaber • Respected Sir
Rhadopis of Nubia • The Search • The Seventh Heaven • Thebes at War
The Thief and the Dogs • The Time and the Place • Voices from the Other World
Wedding Song • The Wisdom of Naguib Mahfouz
Mohamed Makhzangi *Memories of a Meltdown*
Alia Mamdouh *The Loved Ones • Naphtalene*
Selim Matar *The Woman of the Flask*
Ibrahim al-Mazini *Ten Again*
Yousef Al-Mohaimeed *Munira's Bottle • Wolves of the Crescent Moon*
Hassouna Mosbahi *A Tunisian Tale*
Ahlam Mosteghanemi *Chaos of the Senses • Memory in the Flesh*
Shakir Mustafa *Contemporary Iraqi Fiction: An Anthology*
Mohamed Mustagab *Tales from Dayrut*
Buthaina Al Nasiri *Final Night*
Ibrahim Nasrallah *Inside the Night • Time of White Horses*
Haggag Hassan Oddoul *Nights of Musk*
Mona Prince *So You May See*
Mohamed Mansi Qandil *Moon over Samarqand*
Abd al-Hakim Qasim *Rites of Assent*
Somaya Ramadan *Leaves of Narcissus*
Kamal Ruhayyim *Days in the Diaspora*
Mahmoud Saeed *The World through the Eyes of Angels*
Mekkawi Said *Cairo Swan Song*
Ghada Samman *The Night of the First Billion*
Mahdi Issa al-Saqr *East Winds, West Winds*
Rafik Schami *The Calligrapher's Secret • Damascus Nights • The Dark Side of Love*
Habib Selmi *The Scents of Marie-Claire*
Khairy Shalaby *The Hashish Waiter • The Lodging House*
Khalil Sweileh *Writing Love*
The Time-Travels of the Man Who Sold Pickles and Sweets
Miral al-Tahawy *Blue Aubergine • Brooklyn Heights • Gazelle Tracks • The Tent*
Bahaa Taher *As Doha Said • Love in Exile*
Fuad al-Takarli *The Long Way Back*
Zakaria Tamer *The Hedgehog*
M. M. Tawfik *candygirl • Murder in the Tower of Happiness*
Mahmoud Al-Wardani *Heads Ripe for Plucking*
Amina Zaydan *Red Wine*
Latifa al-Zayyat *The Open Door*